EXTRA ORDINARY EXPERIENCES
OF AN

(EXTRA) ORDINARY GIRL

EXTRA ORDINARY EXPERIENCES
OF AN

(EXTRA) ORDINARY GIRL

Authored by
Kiran Tandon

Disclaimer

Registered Office- 907-Sneh Nagar, Sapna Sangeeta Road,
Agrasen Square, Indore – 452001 (M.P.), India
Website: http://www.wingspublication.com
Email: mybook@wingspublication.com

First Published by WINGS PUBLICATION 2022
Copyright © Kiran Tandon 2022

Title: **EXTRAORDINARY EXPERIENCES OF AN (EXTRA) ORDINARY GIRL**
Price: INR 699 / $18
All Rights Reserved.
ISBN 978-93-93966-13-1

LIMITS OF LIABILITY/DISCLAIMER OF WARRANTY

Acknowledgement

The inspiring lot makes the world a better place. What makes it even better are people who share the gift of their time to mentor future generations. Thank you to everyone who strives to grow and help others grow. You never know who might need this or who it could uplift. It is wisely said, "sometimes, *a book could change your life.* "With this in mind, I penned *"Extra Ordinary experiences of an (extra) Ordinary Girl,"* based on real-life events of my mother, Usha.

Writing a book is more challenging than I thought and more rewarding than I could have imagined. And for that to happen, many pillars are involved who supported me through this extremely nostalgic and rollercoaster journey. And I would like to thank each one of them individually.

"I have to start by thanking my awesome husband, Vineet Tandon, for reading early drafts to giving me advice on the story plots and the cover. He was as important to this book getting done as I was. Thank you so much, my heartbeat."

I want to thank my lovely brother Kunal and sister-in-law, Nandni, followed by my beautiful sister, Kanchan, and brother-in-law, Rahul, for sharing their experiences with Mom and providing feedback on the story instances. This book would not have been possible without their support. Thank you so much, my lovelies.

I want to thank my mother-in-law, Rajni Tandon, for helping me share her thoughts on life in the 50s to 70s and helping me imagine plots that were unknown to me. Thank you so much, Mom; I would not have done it without you!

I want to thank my Son, Abeer, and my daughter Shanayaa for their inquisitiveness which let me write the plots well. Thank you so much, my little munchkins. Mom is proud of you!

I want to thank everyone at Wings Publications who helped me so much. Special thanks to Deepak, Kailash, and Abhas. The team was always patient with me.

I want to thank Yogi Kumar for scribbling my mom's portrait and making her come alive on canvas, and Tushar Bhattacharya, Bidhan Bhattacharya, for digitally illustrating an excellent cover design. This cover by Yogi, Tushar and Bidhan is the most incredible cover design I could ever imagine for my book.

I want to thank the Edioak team for crafting a rough piece of coal into a diamond and making the story feel like a movie.

None of this would have been possible without my dear friend, Rakhi Wanchoo, and my guiding angel, Heavena. They were the first people who believed in me and inspired me to write a book. They stood by me in all thick and thins. They indeed proved what true friendship is.

I'm forever indebted to Sanya Parashar, Devraj, Syed Miraj Faredie, Ravgun, and Garv for their help, keen insight, and ongoing support in bringing my stories to life. Because of their efforts and encouragement, I have been able to scribble my mom's life story and pass her legacy to the world, who could draw as much inspiration as I did.

Having an idea and turning it into a book is as hard as it sounds. The experience is both inertly challenging and overtly rewarding. I especially want to thank the individuals who helped make this happen and all the family members and friends.

To my friend, Ritu Jain, for always being the person I could turn to during those dark and desperate times. She was with me in ways that I never knew that I needed.

I want to thank EVERYONE who ever said anything positive or uplifting to me or taught me something. I heard it all, and it meant something.

I want to thank my MOM and DAD for blessing me from Heaven and making this piece of art come alive.

Last but not least, I want to thank God. For bestowing me with courage, for I needed to relive the parts that left a void in my heart, at times, again and again. Without Him, nothing could be possible.

Preface

As the world turned green and new flowers blossomed

In the melodious pining of our hearts,

A quiet yearning found its home

Between words carefully penned into a piece of paper.

Unable to take it any further, it rose and spoke its story out loud;

Beauty emanated from the ordinary, and love found its home.

Our eyes reflect the world we see, and our hearts imbibe the love,

Even if it is from mere words, to feel the rush in our veins.

Love can make one do the most irrational acts,

And love can evoke your innate superhuman.

The power of words holds ice ages and oceans in the o's and the c's

And conveys the world in a four-letter tree.

The tunes are sung on an Aeolian lute

They are more profound and pretentious than most.

Yet, they hold a tranquility in their strings that

When the dainty fingers hum a tune, they dance,

Reciprocating a perfect symphony.

The same grace, ease, and love

get transported through music.

And this love song, a melody to dance,

Intricately sews intimate narratives

Hoping to find a home (even if it is ephemeral) in the corner of your heart.

- Kiran Tandon

When she enters this world, a woman becomes a daughter to someone. She is nurtured within the embrace of her mother. The mother was once like her, this delicate and brimming with wonder. She, too, sat on her father's shoulders once to stare at the much bigger and taller world with glistening eyes, steering away from the crowd; she, too, had felt safe.

Soon, this young girl learns to share, bond, and spread her love by becoming a sister to her younger or elder siblings. She quarrels with them, threatens to spill their secrets to the intimidating father figure, but defends and looks after them. Strength and compassion grow inside her over time, partly by nature's grace and partly as a gift from her mother. And so does her wisdom. She chooses to meet new people, decides on her most sincere connections, and then learns to become a friend, sharing her deepest darkest secrets with her confidant, and not just that - but also her clothes, jewellery, and makeup. The woman learns benevolence, but she may realize that either by choice, circumstance, or both - brought on by sharing or sacrifice.

As she falls in love, she gets married and advances more of everything she knows— compassion, responsibility, quarrelling, and friendship. Basically, she becomes a superwoman until she becomes a supermom. By this time, she had revised her life experiences and her life lessons multiple times. Now she is ready to pass it on to the tiny versions of herself she had created.

Is it not wonderful how women in our lives complete us? They make us who we are and, more importantly, bear, create, and nourish us mentally, physically, and emotionally. No matter what roles they play, they shower abundance, nothing less of the sort. Utter, complete, abundance.

But what happens when this wholesome package has to play the father figure too? What level of struggles and hardships does she have to face? And what level of superabundance does she meets to nourish and nurture her family?

This is the story of one such woman, Usha, my mother. My late mother. Despite being a wonderful daughter, a sister, a friend, a partner, and a mother, what truly defined that woman was her unique personality. She was coy with a temper that could shake mountains. Her silence was powerful, but her words spoke confidence. Her heart, although overtly timid, was covertly rebellious and adventurous.

This woman was independent and free in her spirit, with a progressive mindset. She performed her duties diligently and enabled her kids to settle in prosperous careers and homes.

I firmly believe, and it is evident through world examples, too, that behind every successful woman, there is another woman with her own unique story to tell. I am the result of the web of the beautiful journeys of my mother and those before her. Therefore, in the heartwarming memory of my mother, I bring you this book to celebrate the journeys of all the 'extraordinary women' around us.

INDEX

Chapter

1

The Blessing

Chapter 1
The Blessing

Dayaram hurriedly sat on his bicycle and started pedaling impatiently. He was in a tense state. His heart raced as if he was caught in the chaos. His wife was about to give birth to their third child, and he was still thirty minutes away from them at their dwelling in Paharganj.

Dayaram's sweaty palms struggled to grab hold of the solid handles and his *chappal*[1]. Threatened to fall off, unable to withhold his rushed movements. The tip of his thumb hurt from constantly ringing the bicycle bell, and a wave of regret threatened to wash over him. Dayaram had to leave his pregnant wife unattended to put up tents for a wedding, with a promise to take her to the hospital on time. But, raising three children was no joke, and even if he could travel back in time, he would still have to leave his house that day to make ends meet, for they needed money to run their lives. There was no room for regrets for those who lived in small spaces, so he shook it off.

The wedding had lasted for a few hours and his *thekedar*[2] Would not allow him to leave early without the risk of losing

---

1 Slipper.
2 A supervisor or a boss.

his job. Dayaram had been helpless and agitated the whole time. Picturing his wife waiting for him within the faded blue walls of their house, coupled with the anxious children sitting by her side, petrified him. Finally, after hours of fidgeting, he was able to pack up the tent and was now making his way through the busy roads of New Delhi. He peddled with the vigor of an adolescent boy, but his jittery hands, on the other hand, reflected the dedication and maturity of a grown man. The smooth skin of his face marred by a heavy tan was just like that of any teenager, but the deep crinkle in the middle of his forehead suggested otherwise. Dayaram had to grow up way before it was his time. Societal obligations had led the eighteen-year-old boy towards manhood at a very tender age, and the same went for his wife, who was only fifteen when they had succumbed to the atrocity of child marriage.

As he came close to his house, he felt a tingling sensation in his palms which grew numb from holding on to the bicycle handle. He hurriedly wiped the sweat pouring down his face against his shirt sleeves before parking his cycle outside his house. He rushed inside, walking quickly through the cozy but small living room, and unlocked the bedroom door; it squeaked slightly; he had made a mental note to open it slowly as the noise might wake up his wife. But she was far from asleep. She toppled and turned on the bed, trying to quench the want to scream. Her two kids stood nearby to try their best to assist her. The worry in their faces stood out as if they were caught in a vortex of agony. Before the vortex could deepen and bid danger, the eldest daughter Poorti put up a brave face in front of her younger brother Nishok and said, "Niku, go ask Bihari Lal Chacha for his tempo. Father has come home."

Dayaram hated to admit it, but he had been just as perplexed as his young son upon entering the room until Poorti's words had shaken him out of his trance. He realized that this had not gotten any easier the third time and looked at his eldest child. As a young fellow, he had been nauseous with anxiety when Poorti was on her way into this world, and his mass relatives' eager presence was of no help either. Their excitement, however, had faded away, not over time, but rather instantly upon the announcement of a ladki, a girl, whereas Dayaram had been merely grateful to his newborn daughter for providing rescue from all the overbearing enthusiasm.

A yelp from his wife made him jump immediately at her aid, sliding slippers through shaking swollen feet and helping her get up from the bed. But though he was feeling proud of Poorti's presence of mind, he could not mention it.

'Praising kids gets them overconfident,' he reassured himself as he walked his wife out of their house in a hurry.

The tempo started spewing out smoke from the exhaust pipe. Bihari Lal Chacha sat with Nishok in the passenger seat. A sheet had been placed in a feeble attempt to make the rusted space at the back somewhat comfortable - young Nishok had outdone himself, and suddenly Dayaram could not wait to have another child. After the father and daughter had managed to get Padmavati to mount the vehicle, by innate understanding, Poorti did not follow her family inside the tempo.

"Prepare dinner. Your mother won't be with us when we come back."

With that, Dayaram sat inside the tempo, and Poorti saw the dull red vehicle, with chipped writings, disappear as it steered around the corner.

Her eyes pooled with tears upon getting inside the home. She locked its door and burst into a fit of tears. She wanted to be with her mother, but instead, now she would have to cook food for her entire family.

"I will make the youngest one does all other chores." She said to herself as she wiped her tears and began preparing for dinner.

****

"Please wait outside," a nurse had told Dayaram as his wife was taken away in a wheelchair.

He sat on the bench for a second, only to get up and start packing up and down the lobby the next moment. Noticing his father's restlessness, Nishok brought a glass of water from the water cooler near the reception. His young boy's considerate gesture served as a distraction, and he gladly took it. With eyes resembling that of his own father, Nishok reminded Dayaram of his childhood in Pakistan. He wondered if his own father felt something similar on the day Dayaram or his siblings was born.

If the stoic old man did, Dayaram wouldn't know, for fathers never talked about such things, and being one himself, he understood that. As soon as his birthplace crossed his mind, Dayaram's terror on the day they were supposed to cross the border of Pakistan after the partition of 1947 came along. Half of the trains that migrated innocent civilians ended up in a heap of dead bodies, which was then reciprocated from the other side of the border by another train of slaughtered passengers.

Dayaram and Padmavati had boarded one of many such trains with their two children and, by the mercy of fate, made it alive to India, where they had to start over. Even though the family recovered on the outside, an overpowering fear had been bottled up inside Dayaram, like a matchstick trapped inside a glass bottle hoping to be extinguished by suffocation but forever threatening to set the world ablaze. Unlike the rest of his family, who had shed tears of terror the entire time, Dayaram had maintained a strong exterior and focused on his duty to bring his family to safety. After it was all over, Dayaram never expressed even the least of it, or rather much of anything, avoiding the domino effect from taking over his emotions.

A nurse walked up to him and asked, "Doctor *Sahiba* is asking if the patient has any special conditions?"

Subsiding the death-like pallor on his face, he replied, "She has a neural condition." The nurse nodded and informed him they couldn't give her any anesthesia or painkillers during the delivery as she rushed back inside. Dayaram, being aware of her frail health condition, sighed and sat down to wait for the doctor to come out. His wait seemed forever. He couldn't contain his anxiety and started walking restlessly. A few screams from the hospital sent shivers throughout his body, making his anxiety pounce and multiple manifolds. Fueling his consternation even further, a stretcher with a corpse crossed him, and swiftly, mourning filled the place, reverberating within every nook. All this made Dayaram dizzy, and he sat down with a panic-stricken face.

After several hours, a woman in a white lab coat remarked, "It's a girl," and walked past him quickly without a 'congratulations' or expectations for a reward of any sort.

"These people wouldn't stop asking for *badhai*[3] when my son was born," he thought to himself. The difference was drastic. Nishok's birth had consisted of rejoicing looks from strangers and expressions of relief from the relatives that it had not been another girl. "It's like people hold their breaths for an entire year, and my wife expands while their brains shrink," Dayaram chuckled at his own theory, realizing that the exhaustion from the day was starting to drive him eccentric. He never cared about the gender of his children. He loved his elder daughter immensely even though he was much younger and far less anticipating when she was born; now that he was mature and more than ready, he refused to wait another second before seeing his newborn child.

When a mother holds her baby in her arms, her heart speeds up and slows all at once as it tries to contemplate between euphoria and contentment. It alternates between the two extremities as if it were trying to compose a rhythmic lullaby for the little one. When her husband approached, Padmavati was sleeping, humming a tune, and breathed a sigh of relief. As much as she never wanted to let go of the little one, she also couldn't wait for her husband to hold their baby.

The husband and wife shared a comfortable silence; no words were necessary as she gently handed the child to Dayaram, who supported the baby's head against his forearm. It had been a few seconds of Dayaram standing in the same spot and gazing at his daughter when a tiny frown made its way onto Padmavati's face. Her breath hitched, and doubt

---

3 congratulatory rewards for revealing good news

clouded her mind, along with unsurety regarding the doubt.

'Surely, it cannot be the case. He loves our Poorti after all.'

But a second daughter was a common reason to frown in many families, and Dayaram's slow movements could very well mean displeasure. With that fear in mind, she hesitantly asked her husband," Suno ji, my dear, our household has been blessed with a Devi, a goddess. Aren't you happy?"

This shook Dayaram out of his trance of registering the delicate face of his newborn daughter. Hues of coral and scarlet adorned her form, and he never thought he could stop being appalled at the wonder of nature for creating someone so tender, that too, of his own flesh and blood. The focused look on his face melted into a smile as he looked towards his wife now, his attention shifting to the sheen of prior sweating on her skin because of the hard labor. Her eyes seemed tired, and timidity shone in them, reminding him of her question.

"She has brought light into our lives; how can I be anything but happy? See how her eyes shine." He looks another look at his daughter, seeing her eyes glimmer.

"So do yours," Padmavati replied in a relieved tone, with all her worry disappearing from her mind like the fog that evaporates in the sun upon seeing Dayaram's watering eyes.

He quickly wiped off the fast-approaching tears, avoiding eye contact with his wife, whose expression began to soften. He hadn't realized when he started getting so emotional and handed the baby back to her mother, but not before lovingly muttering,

"Her name will be Usha, our light."

****

In the heart of India resides devotion towards extraordinary goddesses -

The slayer of an arrogant demon king, Durga rides a lion with a trident in her mighty hand:

An epitome of feminine strength. The bearer of spring and music,

Lovable Sarasvati blesses her disciples with wisdom and knowledge.

The liberator of the soul, Kali, bites her tongue,

Suppresses her rage and earns veneration.

And finally, Lakshmi, the bearer of wealth, abundance, and fertility

Chooses to enter only the most welcoming house that is decorated and clean.

In the heart of India resides devotion towards extraordinary goddesses, but in the hands of India resides the stains from their blood.

Lakshmi aayihai[4]. An embodiment of goddess Lakshmi has graced your household," said Bihari Lal, sending a nod in Dayaram's direction.

The two were sitting outside the hospital room, recovering from the previous rush of the drive to the hospital and their anxious anticipation of childbirth. Niku was inside, taking his own time to observe his baby sister. He watched every little

---

4 Lakshmi, an Indian Goddess for money and prosperity, has come.

movement of the baby in fascination, not understanding what the baby did the whole time before coming out. Finally, he placed his fingers near the baby and smiled at how little the baby's fingers seemed near his. Slowly as the silence between them started to set in, the prior rush of adrenaline seemed to come to a rest. Meanwhile, Dayaram's mind was stuck with an instant realization, and hastily, he let his fingers inside the pocket of his wrinkled kurta. He took out some money and handed it over to Bihari Lal.

"Bring some sweets from the nearest confectioner, will you?" He said to Bihari Lal, who grabbed the money hesitantly and put it in his front pocket.

Dayaram expected the man to leave, but he prolonged his stay as if he had something to say. The shared silence had been entirely different for the two of them, Dayaram realized. All this while, Bihari Lal had been fidgeting just like he was doing now, testing his heels on the ground and preparing for his exit.

"Are you sure, Brother?" He suddenly asked, only to receive a puzzled gaze from Dayaram.

"Another daughter is going to prove burdensome to you, and what will people say when they find out you had yet another girl child? It's not too late to resolve it. We are still in the hospital."

The implication was nothing alien to Dayaram. He had first heard it across the border when his eldest child Poorti was born, and here he was, in the presence of reformative yet ineffective laws of India, hearing it yet again. He took a deep breath whilst contemplating his response to something which he couldn't fathom the profaneness of.

"I could not be more certain, Bihari Lal. And since when did goddess Lakshmi become burdensome?" He mocked Bihari Lal's hypocrisy. The irony was epic, after all. The same goddess for whom the doors are left ajar every year on the festival of Diwali, in an instant, turns into an unwelcomed infant when born into a home.

"She had her destiny mapped out from the minute she entered this world, and who are we to take that from her?" Dayaram's tone was soft and affectionate as he talked about his daughter until the usual brusque demeanor appeared once again,

"Now run off and buy those sweets I asked you to."

With that, Bihari Lal shot up from his seat, muttering, "Of course, of course," and strode outside the building as fast as his legs could carry him.

****

The chronology of events following a girl child's birth usually starts with a blasphemous implication, just like the one brought up by Bihari Lal. However, that suggestion has been rejected, and the child emerges to mingle with society; pity is bestowed upon her family by friends and strangers.

When after two days of observation at the hospital, both Usha and Padmavati finally made it home, a quietness of no name prevailed. It was a small house in Paharganj with cemented floorings. It looked humble but radiated life. It was a home they built with love and hard work. Much to his reluctance, Dayaram's *thekedar*[5], had made him rush to work,

---

5 A supervisor or a boss.

and Niku had gone to see off Bihari Lal Chacha. Poorti was in the middle of her afternoon nap, exhausted from managing the household, and her mother thought it best not to wake her up. Placing the sleeping baby down, Padmavati was about to rest her arms when Gauri Mausi entered the house with a *potli*[6] Tucked under her armpit.

Though she was petite, she looked ten years older, and her demeanor was snobbish. Her entrance was dramatic as if sucking every good vibe in the room as a terror on everyone's faces surfaced. Gauri Mausi was the mother-in-law of one of Dayaram's distant cousins, whom they acquainted after they departed from Pakistan. However, she lived nearby but had only visited them once since they had settled.

"Padma, my child, help me with this bundle." She looked at the sleeping baby before handing it over to the exhausted mother sitting on the *veranda*[7]. She wiped her face with the corner of her *kameez*[8] Before fanning it in a rhythmic motion.

"Would you like some water or tea, *Mausi*[9]?"

"Water will be good." Nodding, Padma started walking towards the kitchen.

"Squeeze a lemon in it, child. Oh, and a pinch of salt."

Padmavati assumed that the old lady had heard about the arrival of their baby and was visiting to congratulate the family. Preoccupied with that disposition, Padma entered the room a few minutes later with the demanded beverage in her hand

---

6 A small handbag.
7 A roofed open gallery or portico is attached to the exterior of a building.
8 A long tunic was worn by many people from South Asia, typically with a salwar or churidars.
9 Aunt.

and noticed Gauri Mausi had disassembled the potli.

"Thank you, child. Here you go, do not spend money on new clothes for the girl."

Padmavati found the thoughtful gesture peculiar coming from the woman who had yet to acknowledge her newborn's presence in the room. She looked at the scattered garments on the floor only to find that they were stained and worn out. Before she could overcome her speechlessness, Niku and Dayaram entered the house hand-in-hand.

"Oh, my handsome Krishna *Kanhaiya*[10], he has grown so much since I last saw him."

Taken aback by the overwhelming antics of the strange woman, Niku cowered behind his father and refused to greet the guest. Dayaram walked forward and bent down to touch the feet of the elder.

"*Pai Lagu, Mausi.* It's nice to see you."

The woman gave him a hefty pat on his back and said," May God grant you patience, child. These are tough times." A pall of gloom descended on Dayaram's face as he glanced at his wife. She gave him a discreet nod of disappointment. The couple had understood the reason for their guest's arrival.

"Nishok, go inside to your sister Poorti" Dayaram instructed his young son and sat beside the woman.

She continued speaking," Who can control *kismet* (fate)? You should start looking for a match for Poorti to lessen some of your burden, child."

"I am thankful for fate, *Mausi*. There is no burden, only

___
10 A little God

blessings. Our household seems to be thriving because of our two daughters."

The woman took a pause. It was clear as daylight that Dayaram did not regret the birth of his child, so she took another approach, desperate to make them understand her concern.

"If you think so, child, then you must be right. However, I would suggest not trying for another child after this. Two boys would mean two shoulders to lean on in the future, but another girl would mean the opposite."

Gauri *Mausi* leaned back in contentment. Finally, she had gotten through to the couple. The world was now a better place for her.

Poorti had heard the murmur of conversation and was now sleepily walking into the *veranda*. The guest looked her up and down in disapproval as the young woman made her greetings before walking towards her newborn sister and taking the baby into her arms with a smile.

"It is not appropriate for young women to nap in the afternoon, girl. Your in-laws will not be as lenient as your parents."

Gauri *Mausi* looked towards Padmavati, expecting the mother to join her in the reproach. It was mandatory to shape daughters into enduring beings for their future households, after all.

"Poorti.... Take your sister inside and put a *kaala tceka*, (black mark) on, to ward off evil eye from her." Dayaram intervened. Poorti nodded and rushed inside, wanting to be as far away from the condescending woman as possible.

"*Mausi*, we are very content with our children, be it our son or daughters. You do not need to worry."

Sensing another 'but' from the relentless woman, Dayaram decided to finally end the conversation for good, "Would you like something else, *Mausi*? Doctor *Sahiba*[11] Said that the Padma and the baby need to rest."

"No, nothing. I should get going." Finally, the woman received the cue and was about to walk out the door when Padmavati, who had been quiet throughout the entire exchange, called out, "*Mausi*!"

The woman turned with an inquisitive look on her face, "You forgot your Potli."

****

Tiny hands grab hold of the glob of clay with the mud smearing over chubby forearms and slowly sneak onto the dark blue frock. Dropping the fragment of clay onto the ground with some force, she sat down cross-legged in front of it before working on creating one shape after the other. Usha loved making plates, glasses, bowls, and dolls - everything which allowed the imaginative child to construct a mini household. Something about this activity took away her focus from the rest of the world, and the lack of playmates was a welcoming feeling for the young ceramicist. After spending hours in the sun and skipping her lunch, much to Padmavati's dismay, Usha would only leave her craft when nature started to dim its lighting, marking the approach of the evening. After that, Usha would fidget during the night, struggling to sleep with the anticipation for the clay to solidify. Once that was done, the

---

11 respectful Indian term of address for a woman.

very satisfying painting process was done to bring the objects to life.

On the days when her health wasn't holding her back, Padmavati often joined in to assist the clumsy child with painting her tiny playthings. It was a fantastic bonding activity for the two until the mother's health started deteriorating again, and the child was left to play alone for another couple of days until her mother could join her again. This was an unending cycle, with Padmavati's health condition being an enormous concern for the family.

The oldest one had the unending pressure of managing the household all by herself, while the youngest, who was in the greatest need of a mother, would end up in the care of her inexperienced older siblings while their father would leave to make ends meet. Amid this neglect, Bala Aunty was often a savior in disguise for young Usha: A middle-aged woman who had gotten married when she was fifteen, and her husband passed away, leaving her childless, along with some land passed to her.

"Her skin was a warm beige that glowed under the merciless sun and backdropped all the layers of gold she had dangling from her hands. Her eyes were feline and utterly luminous as if they had projected their ray beams. She had a mole dotted just above her pouting lips and a scatter of freckles all around."

The revenue from the leftover land from her husband was enough to support her lifetime. She always had the same schedule and would wake up every day before the sun showed up. The faint ringing of a tiny bell could be heard if you decided to pass by her house just around the time for breakfast. Her kind eyes held a soft spot for the young Usha, who would play in the mud on the afternoons when Bala would pass their house on her way to the *mandir*[12]. Eventually, the kind lady couldn't resist and started joining Usha during her clay-painting ventures while holding a vague conversation with Padmavati. During the days when Padmavati fell sick, Bala would appear like a mirroring image of the child's mother. But their bond was quite different from how it seemed to be. Despite their age gap, they were like good friends. Usha would often get admonished for addressing Bala by her first name, making Bala aunty raise to her defense, insisting that she preferred it this way.

One quiet afternoon, the two of them were sitting on a *charpai* (traditional woven bed) in the *veranda* with a plate of sharifa (custard apple) resting between them. Usha was savoring the sweetness of the exotic fruit Bala had fondly brought over - one by one, receiving tiny pieces from the grown-up's hands and placing unwanted seeds from the previous bites on them. Bala loved observing the child until some red rashes on Usha's neck caught her attention. Upon further inspection, the rashes seemed to have spread throughout the child's body, and Bala grew more concerned.

"I shouldn't bother her poor mother," she thought to herself, realizing that it was one of those days when Padmavati was unwell.

Bala aunty took Usha to her house and bathed her with disinfectant-infused water. Then, massaging the child's skin with coconut oil, she handed Usha a glass of milk containing turmeric powder, an age-old remedy for allergies and infections.

---

12 Temple.

Usha made a face, but one stern look from the otherwise calm-visaged adult made her gulp down the contents at once.

It wasn't until a few days later that the doctor diagnosed the worsening rashes as chickenpox. With some ointment to relieve the itch from the rashes, the restless child was left to the care of her elder sister and Bala. Due to her low immunity, Padmavati was to maintain a distance from her contagiously sick child. At that time, Usha needed the love and warmth of her mother. The days following that went in excruciating pain. The heartache and abandonment from her mother due to her sickness worsened her well-being.

Gradually, Usha recovered and resumed her daily activities. However, the disease left behind its scars that remained permanently on her face as a souvenir, leaving her disheartened whenever she saw herself in a mirror. But Bala aunty lifted her spirits, calling the disease *'Mata ka Aana'* (blessings from goddess), considering it a blessing in disguise. She said something good is about to happen now, and she has been blessed. Usha embraced her words and, as a beacon of hope, eventually got comfortable in her own skin.

Chapter

2
A Flower to Bloom

Chapter 2
A Flower to Bloom

The morning sun poured its subtle glow on the path leading to the bustling public school. Usha tilted her head toward the ground as something in the soil gleamed a few centimeters away from her worn-out black buckled shoe - a hand-me-down of Poorti's to which Usha had dedicated her entire morning, first wiping it with a damp cloth, followed by a dry cloth. When the results were still somewhat unsatisfactory, a thin layer of kitchen oil was applied. That had done the job, at least for the time being. Unfortunately, the sheen of oil later turned out to be a dust magnet, making it difficult to even opt for the usual method of wiping the dusty shoes against her cloth-covered calves without it sticking to her uniform. Her eyes were mourning her temporary success as she peered at her shoes, but this sadness was soon replaced by curiosity. She found a red bangle on the ground walking towards the gleaming object. This wasn't uncommon as women usually wore those and often lost broken bangles in random places, but this one was completely intact. Usha smiled as she picked it up and slid it on her wrist. Instead of resting securely on her forearm, the circular object glided further up the young girl's lean arm. Tucking it inside her shirt sleeve, Usha rested it on a safe spot, securing it around the flesh of her bicep, and continued on the path to her school. The old shoes had been made up for.

Soon, her daily travel companion joined her, and the two started talking.

"I have been waiting for a while now! What took you so long?" Chanchala kicked a pebble with her foot making Usha glance down at her shoes again.

"Binni and Anku were at each other's throats. It took me ages to break those two apart."

"Well, that explains the hair," commented Chanchala and giggled teasingly, making Usha reach a hand towards her hair in a vain attempt at fixing them and yelling at her in a childish prattle. The Bhatia household consisting of six siblings was ever anything but quiet. After Usha, Dayaram and Padmavati had three more children, and the two youngest ones had formed a habit of picking loving fights during the most unsuitable circumstances. These fights often led to intervening by the older ones, who usually ended up taking sides and quarrelling amongst themselves. Niku had a soft spot for his sister Binita who was the youngest, whereas Poorti was always up for defending the second youngest, her brother Anukool. As a result of this chaos, the middle siblings, Usha and Meena, were always left to break things apart, appearing as scraped warriors at the end of a battle - much like today.

"So, I'm guessing you did not bring a tiffin today, although it was your turn." Chanchala cast her a sideways glance making Usha sigh in exasperation.

"Gosh! I completely forgot. I'm so sorry-"

"Save it. I already told you I don't mind bringing food for the both of us daily. You do enough as it is."

Usha cast her friend a look of gratitude. There was no room was disagreement. It was only eight in the morning, and Usha was already exhausted from her daily chores. Padmavati's health would repeatedly leave her bedridden for days, and the weight of the household fell upon the shoulders of the eldest daughters. On top of doing the dishes, cleaning the house, and getting herself and her younger siblings ready for school, another load of responsibility had fallen upon her recently. There had been a shortage of water supply in the taps of Paharganj residents for the past few weeks, and each household had to stock up their water first thing in the morning, hauling a few buckets from the handpump at the *chowk*[13]. Usha had woken up at four in the morning to carry bucket loads of water to her house.

They were starting to near school, and Usha breathed in relief. Finally, she could act her age for a while.

****

"Four paise for one bottle," the *kabadiwala*[14] Was adamant.

"Ten paise for two bottles, and I will sell all six to you." Usha made her bargain with a puppy face.

"Not happening, kid." He muttered, making Usha shrug with nonchalance and start to walk away. It was a risky trick, the buyer could either stop you or stick to their resolve, but it rarely

---

13 a road junction or roundabout.
14 Scrap dealer.

missed, leading to the latter result on most occasions.

Usha could almost smell the dusky aroma of the rough brown sheet. She could almost feel the sheen of the glue on the name tags.

She needed to buy those things to cover her school notebooks as per the teachers' instructions, and hence she needed the money. Campa Cola bottles were easy to come by at a neighbour's house or somewhere around school, and she decided to try her hand at selling them to the Ragman.

The money she made from selling bottles allowed her not only to buy books but also to put away a sizeable sum that she could give to her father so that he could buy a store in Paharganj.

Usha had dug a hole in the wall in the kitchen, and she used to put all of the coins that she had saved there. She did this because she believed the coins would one day add up to a considerable amount, allowing her father to buy a shop in the Nabi Karim area of Paharganj.

The target was set at two hundred rupees, and she was determined to win at any cost.

Just a single holler away from success, she kept walking forward, refusing to let the hesitancy show in her footsteps until the man called after her.

"Take the ten paise, kid."

Usha was about to beam tremendously at the peak of her success when she was interrupted by a sharp pain in the middle of her forehead. Madam Sarla had hit her with chalk, and the entire class was staring at her. She had dosed off during the session.

"I was trying so hard to wake you up." Mumbled Chanchala with a mouthful of food. The two friends were sitting in the shade of the Ashoka tree, each with a rolled-up *roti*.[15]

Dipping a piece in the *chutney*- a homemade red chili sauce and an unmatched recipe of Chanchala's, she continued. "You mumbled 'ten paise or nothing' when Madam Sarla called your name." Chanchala chuckled as she recalled the appalled expression of their teacher.

"I thought I was done carrying enough buckets for one day." Usha could not help but painfully chuckle along. She had been assigned the punishment duty of watering the plants around campus after school hours.

The children had become immune to Madam Sarla's sharp aims of her broken chalk at them, and therefore Chanchala had enjoyed the entire sequence until it occurred to her that the punishment could not wait to come on a worse day for Usha.

"Don't worry. I will help you." She tried to cheer up her friend, "Moreover, we have home science class after this."

That put a smile of relief on Usha's face. Home Science was her favorite subject way before it was introduced at school.

Her childhood friend Bala Aunty was the source of her know-how of embroidery and knitting. After Meena was born, young Usha found another playmate to replace Bala aunty and would instead visit the kind lady's house partly for the savory bites of *Sharifa*[16] And partly because of their conversations. Bala was a great listener and always had her two cents to add to any

15 A type of flat, round South Asian bread.
16 Custard apple.

discussion. The two had bonded over time through a different activity than clay sculpting. As Bala would spend most of her days either praying or knitting, Usha picked up a tactic for the same. The casual imitation on Usha's part to fill in the gaps in their conversation soon turned into genuine interest, and their casual conversations turned into proper lessons. Bala was now Bala Aunty for Usha, her teacher who instructed the ways of a needle and thread.

The school was nowhere on Usha's list of priorities in the middle of all the familial responsibilities. These obligations made her lose connection with one of her friends, Chanchala, and eventually, she had to repeat her fifth and sixth grades. Chanchala moved two years ahead of her, and they could not spend as much time together as they once did, attending different classes and forming other priorities.

Usha began to pen down her sentiments in her pocket-sized journal so that she could continue to keep her desires known.

She was accustomed to hearing popular Bollywood tunes emanating from the home of Bala Aunty in the evenings.

She grabbed the radio that belonged to her father and tuned it to *Ameen Sayani's* rendition of *Binaca Geet Mala*, a weekly countdown shows of top Hindi film songs. It was well-liked, with millions of listeners. It was the first radio countdown show of Indian film songs and was the most popular radio program in India throughout its tenure. It was the principal source of popular cinema music on the radio for the Indian subcontinent.

Usha would finish all of her tasks by 8:00 pm on Wednesdays, and then she would go to a quiet area with her radio, where she took great pleasure in listening to the top 10 Bollywood songs and making a note of the countdown in her blue diary.

Usha was often the first to answer any questions about the song's position in the charts and popularity, and she always had the lyrics to songs readily available.

Her ability to write paced on to another level as a result of the boost in creativity that she received from music

Eventually, her artistic creativity became her only saving grace as her talent gained recognition from her headmistress. The latter invited Usha to her hometown in Ghaziabad over the weekend to give her free textbooks and knitting material. This trip with Chanchala and her elder brother, Niku, started at 4 am on a Sunday from their residence. The three covered distance of 36 kilometers on foot in eight hours. While her companions were sweaty and exhausted, Usha's face smoldered with renewed confidence with every step she took.

Chapter

3

A New Forever

Chapter 3

A New Forever

Kites flew swiftly in the shimmering sunlight arena of the sky over Paharganj, some in sweet solitude and others battling their companions until their descent. Among the vibrant flock was a red speck with pompoms on its tail whose *dor*[17] Led to a tanned hand adorned in tiny freshly healed cuts and scrapes, probably earned from the same sharp thread he now held.

The weather had been kind that winter afternoon, and Ramesh was never one to be able to resist the opportunity to climb onto the rooftop, sniff out a crashed and wounded paper aircraft, only to tape it up before sending it off into the battlefield again. He had found a somewhat decent kite somewhere in the narrow lanes of the *bastee.*[18] And after a few unsuccessful attempts, his rose-colored aspirant, which was also the only one he had, was now soaring high up.

"Never fails," Ramesh had shrugged proudly, glancing his proud sight sideways at his older brother, who scoffed in approval.

His brown eyes were squinting at the sky as his fingers moved with a gentle precision as he poured all this

---

17 String
18 A slum inhabited by slum people.

concentration towards their slowly approaching purple enemy. The trick was to adjust one's altitude with minimal movement before reciprocating the opponent's march. Ramesh held his breath in anticipation, his one hand securing its grip on the dor and the other making sure there were no tangles in the rest of the thread beside him. Until a girlish squeal made him look elsewhere. -

Usha balanced the heap of damp clothes on her one arm, awkwardly tilting her head sideways to press against it while she tried to rest the upright *charpai*[19] On its four feet. She let out a sigh of relief when she finally dumped the cold heap on top of the *charpai*, then let out another one of frustration when she noticed a darker circular spot on her black *kurti*[20]. Laundry was her infinitesimal favorite job.

Reserved for the whites, a wire of cumulated cotton string hung from two rusted iron nails blushing at each other from the paradoxical corners of the terrace. She got to work, hoping the sun would stop scintillating and eliminate the clammy sensation. The aerial tournament was good entertainment, and she watched two kites passionately waltzing together before one great dip towards the ground. Usha bent down to pick up the last few garments and inverted the charpai to stand upright once again before hanging them on its two wooden legs. All done.

Reaching for her *dupatta.*[21], which hung from the now

---

19 Cot.

20 A tunic or shirt or a tie is worn especially by women in South Asia.

21 A length of material arranged in two folds over the chest and thrown back around the shoulders, typically with a salwar kameez, by women from South Asia.

occupied wire; she rested it on her shoulders, intending to climb downstairs, but the wire snapped, and the clothes crashed down on the dusty floor of brick and cement. Usha let out a mixture of a gasp and squeal, "Not the whites!"-

Her skin shimmered like a golden firefly against the black night of her kurta, and her raven hair parted in the middle. She wore a tired frown which saddened him for some reason but chose to focus on the hilarity of her predicament. She had taken a jump, or rather a hop, backward as the wire snapped and had not moved a muscle since except for a frustrating facepalm thirty seconds ago. Instead of collecting the dried garments from the floor, she lightly stomped away in dismissal and disappeared into the downstairs doorway. Ramesh felt perplexed until she returned a few seconds later, now heavily stomping in defeat, picked up the clothes and took them with her, probably for another rinse.

Ramesh chuckled at the girl's silly conduct before dragging back his attention to his kite to finish the aerial combat for good, only to find out that he had been holding a loose string all this time. His rose-colored apprentice had crashed, God knows when.

Usha appeared like a lost in her world kind of girl who dressed simply. She looked gorgeous, even when sweating and doing chores. She did not let the sun affect her spirits. On the contrary, she shone brighter than the sun. Her dark eyes searched for something, revealing a curious soul's identity. Her illustrious sun-kissed skin exuberated her youth that left him enchanted. The awkward face and the smile with nervousness made him intertwined in a web of spells she seemed to have cast at that moment. The childish behavior of wooing his kite made him think she was just like him. Maybe for him too? At that moment, something changed on both sides.

****

Kashvi Bhabhi's arrival in the Bhatia household was mainly announced by the tiny jingling bells of her anklet or the savory aroma of her home-cooked *besan laddoos*.[22], steaming hot, wrapped up in a newspaper and a thick cotton napkin. Over the three-ingredient delicacy which melted in your mouth and a cup of *chai*[23], there was a reciprocation of words between the two households' daughters-in-law.

"Mustard oil in curd?" grimaced Anita, "I don't like the sound of that."

"But you like how my hair shines, don't you? Lose that expression. I don't love it either, but it works," Kashvi admitted nonchalantly.

"Oh, alright, alright. I'll give it a try."

During one of many such conversations, Kashvi Bhabhi brought up a suggestion.

"...Sanjeev's cousins, my *devars*[24] Who visits us from Daryaganj every day" she said with a smile that reached her eyes.

Usha was now a young woman in her early twenties, and her family was looking for a suitable match for her to wed. The diligent girl had made her way through all these years by growing up beautifully, both inside and out. Her dark hair

22 An Indian sweet.
23 Tea.
24 Husband's younger brothers.

flowed smoothly to her waist, brushing the corners of her rich arched eyebrows and glowing pink cheeks while she worked ardently at embroidering a garment. Although her features still reflected a childlike innocence, her eyes gave off womanly intelligence as she continued decorating her handiwork which, once completed, she would sell in the market. In various crevices around the house could be found the rewards of her craft, which her clever self-had lovingly saved for an hour of need or perhaps to unburden her father from some of the expenses of her wedding in the future.

As Usha grew young, Dayaram always expressed that he wanted to get free from worldly responsibilities after his kids were married and settled. Subconsciously, Usha was prepared to get married. At the same time, she dreamt that she would have her own house and a loving partner. And together, they will build a beautiful kitchen and decorate rooms. Her father and brothers would no longer restrict her. She will be a free bird to live a life of her choice.

Usha pulled the needle heavenwards while her sister-in-law, Anita's neighbour and friend, continued, "Rooplal *tayaji's*[25] sons, their names are Ramesh and Subhash. Such hardworking boys! They lost their mother at a very young age. Their grandmother did a lovely job raising those two, but now that the generous woman has passed away, some responsibility must also fall on us. So, the brothers come over daily for an afternoon meal they cannot make for themselves. They are sincere young men and well-mannered too! They always offer to help around the house and are very respectful to everyone.

---

25 Dad's older brother.

Woh kehte hein na[26] So they say, 'It is the terrible typhoons that yield the most tenacious trees."

Anita nodded before asking the mandatory question before any Indian arranged marriage, *"Lardka Karta kya hai?*[27]*"*

And so, the two motherless boys were discussed until the sun announced its nap by dimming the lights and tucking itself into the horizon that evening. Then, unfortunately, their mother lost her life due to some medical condition. A shared misfortune commonly brought an understanding between two families when arranging a marriage.

"Ramesh has a business of tailoring materials and sells them to tailors in West and Central Delhi," nodded *Kashvi Bhabhi.*

"Does he make enough for a living?" Anita murmured.

"Enough?" Kashvi bhabhi scorned her question.

"He earns quite good, *bhabhi ji.* Both boys are very skilled. Rooplal Tayaji has passed impeccable earning skills to both his sons. I think it will be a great match. After all, our Usha is quite talented too."

"Oh, I see. Usha is lucky, then. Good for her. She will live a happy life. I pray that this union gets finalized then," Anita's reply brought a grin to her face as she thought about it.

Finally, a meeting was fixed for the following Sunday afternoon when the boys usually hung out for lunch.

****

---

26 So, they say
27 What does the boy do for a living?

The next day, cracking open the groundnut shell between her thumb and index finger, Anita Bhabhi sat on the *charpai* waiting for the guests. She had decided to make the best of the lookout for her sister-in-law by enjoying some peanuts while she was at it. She took the seeds on one of her palms and rubbed the other against them, then softly blowing at the now separated peanut skin, she slowly gnawed at the seeds. Usha, who had been informed about the mission behind Anita Bhabhi's Sunday trip to the *chhat*[28], kept glancing at the stairs at the slightest of sounds.

When it got to the point where she was sure her brain was hallucinating the pitter-patter of footsteps, she decided to focus on brainstorming ingenious and new ideas for her following SUPW lecture at the school the next day. The principal had offered her employment a few months ago after concluding that her skills were adept, and Usha always looked forwards to her time with the curious sixth and eighth graders who seemed to relish their time at crafting after the entire day of sticking their noses inside textbooks.

But it wasn't just Usha who had been made aware of the setup. Kashvi Bhabhi had given the boys a heads up as they walked in that day. And Ramesh knew exactly to whom these references are attached.

"Ab kaisa lag raha hoon?" How do I look?" joked Ramesh as he splattered his face with water in the kitchen before wiping either of his cheeks against his shirt-covered shoulder. Ramesh was a charming young man, full of love and wit. His mother passed away when he was a young child, which brought him under his

---

28 Terrace.

grandmother's care. Life taught him to live by making the best use of the available resources. He learnt the art of business from his father and brother. When he was nine years, he sold out candles outside a school to make up for food and his living. Nevertheless, as an adult, his wit and intelligence aided him in becoming successful very soon. Kashvi and Subhash shook their heads at his antics while he dramatically exited the kitchen, but not before discreetly dipping his fingertips in the *katori*[29] of mustard oil.

The oil that he rubbed on his hands being deeply absorbed by the tissues of his skin, he hurriedly applied some to the ringlets on his head and the remaining all over his face. He tucked his shirt into his pants and then untucked it. Too obvious. Gulping his nervous saliva into his drying throat, Ramesh walked out into the sunny battlefield with no intention of war in his mind.

If it wasn't the unusual sheen of the kitchen oil on his face or the lack of a hollering invite for Subhash as he climbed the steps, then the pristine condition of the freshly purchased kites resting beneath the staircase gave Ramesh away to his brother. Subhash had a good sense of not following his sibling that afternoon.

The wooden roller started its path over a tiny circular dough while the Bhatia men discussed their neighbour's proposal.

"How old did you say the boy was again?" Dayaram questioned his son.

"Twenty-six, daddy Ji, " Nishok replied, recalling the information his wife provided him.

---

29 A bowl.

The roller went back and forth as Anita Bhabhi made another *chapati*[30] While Usha spread ghee on them and placed them in a cotton napkin with her squishy, petal-like fingers, back and forth went the roller, and so did Usha as she went out to serve *chapatis* to the family, caught a conversation whiff, and returned again. She reckoned that she should be a part of it but did not dare to interrupt the father and the son. Sensing her restlessness, Anita tried to dislodge Usha, shaking her out of her attempts to listen to the discussion from the kitchen.

"I know better than the both of them combined, you know," Anita said in a suggestive tone.

Usha blushed at *Bhabhi's* teasing smile and finally admitted, "I feel like walking on the tip of the sword with a deep ocean on either side, feeling both nervous and excited. I just want to know what they think of him to decide what I should think of him."

"Well, for starters, his name is Ramesh, and you can decide tomorrow afternoon when he is flying that red kite of his two houses away, and you see him coincidentally because I never said anything to you."

Usha blinked once, then twice, until it finally registered. She laughed and then hugged Anita *Bhabhi.*[31].

This led Usha to stand just above the stairs and right before the entrance to the chhat the next day. She could neither conclude that this was unnecessary, turn around and go back, nor could she step out in the open when everyone, including the boy, was aware that their families were discussing their

---

30 A thin pancake of unleavened whole meal bread cooked on a griddle.
31 Sister-in-law.

engagement. Therefore, she cleverly picked a hiding spot right behind the doorframe from where she planned to sneak one glance and leave. It was a tricky business. She had to watch in front of her, and behind her, in case a family member decided to sneak up on her.

A lean male figure, for once unaware of being watched physically ignoring his intuition, stepped near the ledge. He had quite a good supply of red kites from his purchase a few days ago and was suspending the one he had decided to name Rosy (in fact, he called all of them Rosy when he replaced the previous one) from the ledge before pulling tactfully at the *dor* and setting it to flight. It was his lucky day because as soon as Rosy climbed high, she was ambushed by an enemy.

Usha had only planned a glance, but she was intrigued half by his excitement over keeping his kite afloat and half by how he was succeeding. He vigorously moved his arms as he tried to pull at the *dor*, resulting in a few cuts here and there, yet he relentlessly persisted.

"He seems to be winning," a voice whispered behind her, and Usha shrieked in surprise.

"Bhabhi!" She whined, partly annoyed and wholly mortified. Staggering to grab her posture,

Anita Bhabhi crossed her arms and impatiently tapped one foot on the ground," So?"

Usha blushed, realizing that she wanted an answer, "He seems nice."

Ramesh instantly recognized the girlish sound that tickled him unusually, which somehow resulted in him letting go of the *dor.* Having found no one on the *chhat* two houses away, he was now hopelessly staring into the sky where Rosy was still sinking at a distance.

"This woman is going to rob me someday." He complained in a whisper, helplessly hoping for it to be real, and stared deep into the dazzling blue sky, unable to conceal his smile.

****

Turmeric stains your rosy palms,

Your doe-like shins, your moonlight arms,

Your simple feet in a silver paraat[32]

Your skin glows like the light of dawn

The liquid gold glides into your heart

You shall love like a woman now.

One of India's age-old traditions has been marrying into one's caste, and the Bhatia's wanting not to be strangers to the concept. Roop Lal Bhatia picked the suit material for his son, a hound's tooth pattern in a twill weave structure, and started preparing his son's wedding attire. His hands shook a little in his unusual attempt at impeccability as he paused every two minutes to check his progress for errors.

Every time a shadow passed him, the furrow between his brows would disappear, and his rigid stance would turn outwardly nonchalant. Roop Lal was a man of few words who wanted his actions to speak louder. Words would come out of

---

32 A large flat plate

his mouth in somewhat of a stumble, requiring twice as much attention, one for his unusual abandonment of silence and second for being able to comprehend his speech. For someone with a few words and even fewer outward displays of emotion, Roop Lal was stitching a suit as he would for anyone and on any other day, but his failed attempts at concealed sighs of sentimental thought said otherwise. He missed his wife more than his boys could ever miss their mother.

Dayaram Bhatia found himself in a similar situation as Padmavati passed away soon after Usha and Ramesh's engagement in 1975. It had been almost a year of grieving before a decision had to be made about continuing the wedding preparations. This was how Dayaram found himself sorting through design samples for wedding invitations. The colors and patterns were hardly differentiable for a man who opted to wear a white *kurta-pyjama*[33] most days. He had dozed off, the leaflets gradually slipping out of his hand, same as his thoughts, until he was interrupted by his daughter's blasphemous utterance,

"Dil aur Teer usme U aur R. (Cupid's arrow through a heart with our initials, 'U' and 'R' inside of it)"

said Usha dreamily before she dodged a dull blue object with the indentations of three toes and a heel on its surface. Dayaram had shot his *chappal* in his light slumber.

Owner of a flourishing catering business and a hardcore follower of the Arya Samaj, a Hindu society with the motto of making the whole world noble and also succeeding it with

---

33 A long shirt and baggy pants with a drawstring at the waist are usually worn by Indian men.

his children, Dayaram was a man of principles. His tough demeanor and stern eyes holding consistent skepticism was an ever-present feature, not just for the distant world but also for his own family. He would criticize and condemn the actions of the government, the judiciary, the owner of the *kiryana store*, the neighbours, and the six of his children, all too frequently. His success in the catering business was a result of the same cautious and perfectionist approach that he hoped to imbibe into his son Nishok as he worked beside him. Quick on their feet, the father and son made a good team and proved to be successful wedding planners for Usha.

Around this time, the Prime Minister announced a state of emergency, which meant that the nation was currently in a precarious situation. At large gatherings like weddings, civilians were permitted to offer potatoes and meals made with potatoes.

Dayaram wanted to serve a three-course meal with a variety of delicacies at Usha's wedding.

Dayaram has built strong ties with his clients due to his many years of experience in the electrical contracting industry and his work in various homes and businesses. For example, one of the clients had been instrumental in securing the necessary authorization for him to serve a sumptuous dinner to fill in the hearts and minds of guests along with their stomachs for his daughter's wedding.

"I don't see any *ladoos*[34] on display" Dayaram caught Nishok by surprise with a smack at the back of his head, and he stumbled before composing himself, knowing the clumsiness

---

34 An Indian sweet.

would add to the skinny yet sturdy man's annoyance. But, instead, everything about Dayaram sought obedience, and Nishok's perplexity led him to wonder if it was his father's focused eagle eyes, his recurring kurta pyjama, or his booming voice which caused him to stammer in response.

"Uh... They are on the far end of the table-" Nishok made a meek attempt at defense but uttered a quick,"-I'll put them in the Centre" when shot with a glare and dashed.

It was in that moment of solitude, having stepped back from the rush of arrangements, when Dayaram's glare melted into a soft look that would go unnoticed by the guests who were focused on dousing his daughter's youthful face with trinkets of turmeric paste. The *Haldi Ceremony35* Marked the approaching of the wedding, and Usha sat on a little stool, surrounded by young and older women who sang,

"Maa meri menu charkha ditta

My mother gifted me spinning wheel

Vich charkhe de mekhan -

it has nails in it...

Maa rani menu yaad payi aave

My benevolent mother, I miss you

Jad charkhe val vekhan.

Whenever I look at this spinning wheel"

****

---

35 Indian pre-wedding ceremony.

The cool breeze fluttered Usha's hair on her face. A ray of sun shone on Usha, which glittered her face like gold adornment among hidden treasures by reflecting her mother's smile. Dayaram felt an unusual tug at his heart, and silent prayer escaped him as he looked heavenwards. Padmavati had given her blessing.

The nearby school football ground was converted into a wedding venue. The floor of the ground was covered with red and black carpet. The large walls were made from the tent house with floral designs. Ornate furniture, statues of beloved deities, candles, chandeliers, and red and golden fabrics made the venue appear like a fairy tale. The Centre of the ground was kept open from the top as it was a place wherein a mandap or altar (a covered structure with pillars) was built. A spot wherein bride and groom will actually perform the wedding nuptials.

The Agni in the holy havan danced in merriment and then composed itself with dignity. Switching between those two actions, it stood ready to purify the occasion and the lives of the pair, to burn the old and pave the way for the new. Sitting in its golden glow, a priest with a luminous forehead scanned the necessary ingredients for the ceremony - ghee, sandalwood, mango leaves, jaggery, turmeric, incense sticks, *gangajal*[36] And a *Diya*[37]. He was wearing an apricot dhoti and a shawl over his shoulders that fell onto his back while the front of his torso stayed bare. Near the priest sat Ramesh in his perfectly tailored suit, long collared shirt, and well-concealed excitement. The fire flickered once again, wanting to glance at Usha's glorious face and straightened up in reverence, much like the men

---

36 The water of Holy River, Ganges.
37 A small oil lamp.

sitting at the *mandap.*[38] As the bride was about to enter.

The base of her maroon sari brushed against the floor as she walked, the *zardozi.*[39] On it shimmering at the smallest of movements. Hues of purple reflected in the radiant garment as if in a vain attempt to break the entrancement of the onlookers, only to be adding to the mesmerism instead. A colossal *bindi*[40] On the middle of her forehead, just a little above her perfectly arched brows, which would turn out to be her signature look for a very long time, seemed like a heavenly orb against her luminescent countenance.

She was walking under a *phoolon ki chadar.*[41] Held over her head from its four corners by her family members, meant to be a symbol of a sheltered life under her family's care. It was bittersweet for Usha to be wobbling up to organize her thoughts. Her previous life seemed to wave at her - the one she was ready to let go of but already missed its familiarity.

The bride and groom sat in front of the fire altar, facing the east, while the *pandit.*[42] Started softly, uttering the *shlokas*[43]. Next, grains, ghee, and gur were offered to the fire to embellish the couple, followed by other sacred offerings. Finally, with the loose end of Usha's sari tied to the end of Ramesh's scarf, they encircled the holy fire seven times, tying the marriage knot.

****

---

38 A temporary platform set up for weddings and religious ceremonies.
39 Embroidery worked with gold and silver threads.
40 A decorative mark was worn in the middle of the forehead by Indian women, especially Hindus.
41 A canopy of flowers.
42 A Hindu priest.
43 A category of verse lines that have spiritual meaning.

She politely nudged her husband's shoulder with the bunched-up stash of cash a week after the flower-decorated taxi had landed the couple in Shiv nagar, where Roop Lal, through his hard-earned savings, had bought a piece of land for the newlyweds.

Seven hundred rupees was what the wedding envelopes had kindly bestowed upon the young woman, who, in turn, lovingly decided to place it on her husband's palm only to pause in hesitance and aim for his arm instead. Faith shone in her thick water-droplet-shaped eyes as they met with Ramesh's before looking away with an unshakeable shyness - it had only been a few days since the newlyweds started interacting after all. Unfailingly puzzled by her actions since the day he saw her, he tilted his head quizzically, making her hesitation grow into nervousness.

When Usha realized his confusion and reluctance, she finally said, " Use this for your business, " extending the money to him.

Ramesh looked at his wife's determined eyes and recalled that girl from the terrace who jumped in surprise at a snapping laundry wire. Unacquainted with her courageous side, he asked her, "Are you sure?"

A silent understanding passed between the two as Usha's hand lingered midair, steely with insistence. Ramesh smiled softly with gratitude, taking in the redness of the *sindoor*[44] (vermillion). On her scalp. Her hair was parted at the center and the pigment extended to the middle of her head in prayer for

---

44 A traditional red or orange red colored powder from India, usually worn by married women along the parting of their hair.

her husband's long and healthy life. Her scarlet ivory bangles shook on her wrists as she shook the money as a reminder, and he finally took it from her wife's red-stained hands, the Alta still blushing in its freshness on their surface.

That night, Usha's husband put the money inside a small wooden box, intending to invest it in better tailoring material, but not before bending his forehead and touching it softly against the palm holding cash - a gesture of reverence to his wife and gratitude towards his fate. Then, he turned around and looked at Usha, who stood coyly against the wall near their bed. He beamed as he pondered, visualizing what a new forever has in store with this fantastic woman, who herself isn't aware of her greatness.

Chapter

4

The Love Lullaby

Chapter 4
The Love Lullaby

A silent tear slid down, marking its agony as a wet trail throughout her face from her fatigued eyes. A shaky breath escaped her chapped lips as she peeked at her swollen belly through her eyelashes. She abruptly yearned for sleep to dismiss her pain, but it was beyond her grasp. It had been two weeks since Usha had been brought into the hospital, and even after fifteen days of experiencing labor pains, the little one still refused to let go of its mother. Unable to tolerate another minute of the fan's maddening whirring sound, which was onsetting headache; she opened her eyes wide with great difficulty looking around the hospital room. A white patch of chipped paint on the mint wall greeted her, and she turned her head towards the visitor's bench, only to find Ramesh sleeping on its uncomfortable wooden surface. Hesitantly, she cleared her throat of its coarseness before calling out for him.

Ramesh stirred in his sleep but did not wake up. He had been bargaining for the lowest price on quality fabrics the entire afternoon before running to catch the bus, which made all his perspiration evaporate like nothing in the cold November air. At first, he had been exempted from the business by the family, for he had to attend to his wife, but after a week, he knew he had to return to work. Worry ate away at his mind the entire time he spent away from his struggling wife, so he took over the job of importing the materials, which would allow him to leave as soon as he brought in the purchases, compared to attending to the customers the whole day until the store closed. It was an exhausting task that he and Subhash usually took turns carrying out, but he welcomed the weariness over the anxiety of leaving his wife unattended. He had rushed to the hospital with his stomach grumbling with hunger from having skipped lunch in the absence of his wife's lovingly packed lunch box. Roop Lal, having had no sisters as a child, lost his wife too soon, who left him with two sons and no daughter, had hardly experienced a feminine influence in his life, nor had his sons. Apart from Ramesh and Subhash's grandmother, whom they knew when they were very young, the family of three men had gotten by well enough for many years. But during the past year, things had changed, and now, the three men, who had become accustomed to Usha holding together the functioning of the household even during her pregnancy, were struggling to make do.

The setting sun entered through the open window spreading its soothing peachy rays. Usha cast another glance at the fan as if glaring at it would magically shut it off. Her husband looked exhausted, and she was reluctant to wake him up before a thought struck her, and she called his name again, "Suno ji, Ramesh...?"

This time, her effort paid off as Ramesh lazily opened his eyes before looking vigilantly towards his wife, "You are awake."

"Have you eaten?" Women, in general, invariably locate the quintessential aspect in any given situation, and Usha's hunch was absolutely right. The men were supposed to dine at Kashvi

Bhabhi's kitchen in her absence, and Ramesh had been sitting in starvation by her side for God knows how long.

"That's not important. How are you feeling? The doctors said that they might be using forceps for the delivery. You should be out of here soon." His concerned voice relieved her of the pain before the doctors could.

Ramesh had gone straight in the direction of her wife's bed upon entering the hospital before retracing his path and looking for the doctor first. He wanted to have some kind of positive news to convey to her.

"I feel tired, but other than that, I am fine." Usha readily left out the part about feeling numb from all the pain and her throbbing headache, which made her eyes shift towards the fan once more, "You should go to Sanjeev Bhaiya's house. Kashvi Bhabhi must have prepared dinner for you. Come back to me after you have eaten."

Ramesh seemed reluctant, but he knew he needed to eat. A wave of nausea seemed to creep up on him as an indication of his body's need for food., so he complied. Taking her wife's hand in his, he looked at her with concern while she mustered up the best expression of reassurance she could. Ramesh sighed with resignation, "I will be back in no time."

Usha nodded, and he gave her hand one final squeeze before getting up to leave. Right, when he was about to exit the room, she called out, "Please shut off that noisy fan before you leave." Several days passed similarly, with Ramesh not letting his guard down for even one second.

****

Meanwhile, there was this Jagjeevan, a fascinating character whose path often crossed with Roop Lal. He walked with a limp and would stand at the threshold of a room, neither fully entering enough to have a round conversation nor leaving altogether to let you off the hook. Standing there, he would talk about his favorite topics, which routinely comprised complaining about his joint pain, the spike in market prices, methods to improve digestion, and wise adages from his wife. He was a widower and one of those people who lived with a constant regret of taking someone for granted and concealing it with the excuse of missing them.

"Don't be so hard on the children,' she used to say." It was that time during the evening when there was the least activity in the bazaar (market). The customers would be focused on grabbing a bite and gravitating toward the food stalls, and the same went for the shopkeepers eating their lunches. Jagjeevan was standing, once again, at the threshold of Roop Lal's shop opposite his own confectionery store. Roop Lal, who had just returned from his lunch, was now standing in front of a fabric-covered table, chalk in hand and a measuring tape around his neck, while his good friend started his ranting.

"I was always nitpicking at my son." Jagjeevan shook his head in dismay before continuing, "I have stopped now, but she isn't here to see it, is she?" He left a pause as if he were expecting a reply.

He clicked his teeth together and scratched the back of his neck whilst staring at the ceiling before he continued, "The other day, he bought them apples for a whole rupee costlier than I would have, but I ate them without a single word of complaint."

He smiled proudly, "The prices of apples, however...." His ranting never seemed to come to a halt.

Jagjeevan's trips to Roop Lal's shop were frequent and uneventful. He would linger right at the entrance and provide the fellow adult with his daily rant, not minding the unwilling eavesdroppers: Ramesh and Subhash. He was a simple man going through the usual complications of life - loneliness, finicky antics driving loved ones away, longing for the company of his deceased wife yet fearing death every single day, and the quintessential desire to play with his grandchildren before his final departure. It was another one of his regular visits on a cozier November afternoon in 1977 when, after the usual greeting of 'Ram Ram!', Roop Lal diverted his eyes from his guest as he always did. A few seconds later, when Roop Lal had finally pulled the thread from the needle, he relaxed his squinting eyes, and the odd silence began to register in his mind. When he glanced towards the visitor, to his surprise, he found Jagjeevan sitting on one of the chairs they had recently installed for the customers inside the shop. The business had bloomed ever since his younger son and daughter-in-law had contributed an auspicious investment which the newly-weds saved from their wedding endowments; and now, due to the inflating income, they were making gradual upgrades to the shop such as improving the countertops, adding a storage cabinet, or those chairs one of which was occupied by Jagjeevan at the moment. Roop Lal returned to the present situation and shot a questioning look at his friend.

"Almighty has gifted me with a granddaughter, friend," exclaimed Jagjeevan in a breathy tone. He seemed like a man with a newfound desire to live, a man who looked forward to going home at the end of the day, a man with a purpose, a man who did not linger in thresholds anymore.

Roop Lal took a long look at his friend and responded with an excrescent nod. Jagjeevan sat with a trembling jaw, clicking his teeth together before he added, "There is a *puja*.[45] Tomorrow morning. *Bahu* (Daughter in law) will be making lunch. I would like it if you could join us."

Ramesh and Subhash exchanged a look - they knew there was no way Roop Lal would be visiting Jagjeevan's house anymore. Their father was a kind man who had always been solicitous about his mother, wife, and daughter-in-law; however, there was a permanent precept about visiting a house with daughters instead of sons. It was difficult to tell whether it was out of consideration of not inflicting further burden upon a family who had the responsibility of tending to its unmarried daughters or if it was out of pure prejudice. But Roop Lal would simply not visit, or if circumstance made him, not accept a single sip of water from a household with daughters.

Deep in thoughts, Subhash felt miserable about losing his mother at a tender age. The scar was too deep to be uprooted, and it engraved itself like a stubborn stain within the walls of his heart. No matter how hard he tried to get over it, it only grew on him day by day. He was barely five years old &his younger brother, Ramesh, was a little over two years old. They were raised by their grandmother, who tried her best to fend off lovelessness.

---

45 Ceremonial worship.

The early childhood days —when kids wanted cuddles from their mom, they learnt to sleep alone, when they were asked to write an essay on "my mom," they didn't know what to write, and it used to onset a hurricane inside their innocent hearts. Subhash knowing, he has a younger brother, grew very protective of him and started being concerned about him. They also grew up hating God as they never understood why such entity would take away their mom from them. So, Ramesh and Subhash grew up to be fiercely independent & little distant too.

Roop Lal gave another gentle nod to his friend without looking up from his work, either too busy to respond or too dismissive to consider. Jagjeevan, who was utterly lost in his own euphoria of contentment, failed to notice the lack of response and went on about the market prices once again before bidding his leave for the day.

Nobody noticed the tornado of turmoil inside Ramesh's mind that day. In other words, even if they did, nobody spoke of it. Usha was nine months pregnant, and although Ramesh would be wholeheartedly grateful for their first child, irrespective of its gender, he was infinitely troubled about her father's reception.

"Dharti pe utar aaya Chanda

tera chehra bana

The Moon has descended upon this soil and climbed into our arms.

Champe ka salona guldastaa

tan tera bana

A bouquet of flowers of Magnolia makes up her form."

After an exhausting process, profound harmony touched Usha's soul as she was lying on the hospital bed. The past couple of hours had been more excruciating to her than her past twenty days put together. Finally, the relief was set in after her tough delivery with forceps as the room reverberated with calm serenity, with its only sound coming from Ramesh's whispered singing towards his newborn daughter. He glanced lovingly at the radiant rosy glow of his baby, whose eyes were still closed, and continued his singing.

"Komal titli meri laadli

O my daughter precious,

Like a butterfly, you are mellow

Heere ki kani meri laadli

A diamond's droplet of luster

O aas Kiran jug jug tu jiye

Nanhi si pari meri laadali

May you keep shining forever,

My treasure, my little angel. "

With that, Ramesh scooped his daughter closer to himself, and the baby licked his beard. She had recognized her father.

This was the sight Usha was graced with when she opened

her eyes, and it was at that moment when she saw Ramesh holding their child with the utmost affection; she felt the love in her growing for her husband alongside the motherly love for her baby. She listened to Ramesh's song, which was almost reduced to soft humming by now before her husband caught her staring.

The two exchanged a smile, too overwhelmed for words, before Ramesh swiftly walked over to Usha and gently handed over the child to her. To recall the twenty days of turmoil that she went through sent chills down her back but much to Usha's astonishment, at that moment, she realized that she would go through it all over again if it meant holding her daughter in the end. Between the two people who had both gone through a rough childhood, words could not suffice to express their feelings about the infant. Silent promises echoed inside the heads of both parents, who swore to give a better life to their kids. The silence only lasted for so long, and Subhash, Sanjeev, and his wife Kashvi entered the hospital room rejoicingly.

"Look how she's glancing around the room," Sanjeev said to his wife before exchanging a congratulatory hug with the new father.

"Reminds me of my daughter when she was only this much. They grow up so fast," said Kashvi Bhabhi, looking in Usha's direction just as Subhash reached out to hold his newborn niece.

The two women exchanged looks, a mutual joy of experiencing motherhood until they were interrupted by a joyous remark made in a pensive tone.

"Usha ki Kiran," remarked Subhash as he observed the baby, "She is a beam of light, a Kiran, brought forth by the dawn that is Usha."

"Indeed, brother. Usha ki Kiran, Usha's Kiran she is." agreed Ramesh, and an adjoined thought hit his head, and he declared the child would be Kiran. Everyone welcomed the decision with a complacent smile.

Once the guests had spent congratulating the new parents and meeting the child, a wave of repressed fret started surfacing and seemed to wash over all the room occupants. A look was exchanged between the three men until one of them finally decided to break the silence, "Is he not coming?" Ramesh sounded dejected. He was aware that there was a chance that his father would be displeased about it being a girl child, but he hoped that the older man would come around for the sake of his first grandchild.

"Have patience, brother. He must be on his way." Subhash consoled him whilst Sanjeev nodded in agreement.

With Kashvi seated beside Usha's hospital bed, the women were talking amongst themselves whilst the men sat huddled together, trying to keep Usha away from the knowledge of her father-in-law's probable reaction to the child.

Eventually, a conciliation talk was planned with Roop Lal before he could have a confrontation with Usha to spare the weary mother.

The three men excused themselves as they walked out into the corridor, bracing themselves for a debate only to pause in their footsteps.

Roop Lal was already walking in their direction with a smile and a box of *jalebis.*[46] in hand. As he walked closer, he took out one of the twisted orange delicacies and shoved it in Ramesh's mouth, which was already gaping with shock. The other two laughed with incredulousness at the surprising turn of events, making Ramesh shake out of his stupefied trance before following the impatient Roop Lal, who couldn't wait to greet his granddaughter, into the hospital room.

Holding little Kiran in his hands, "She will be our Kiran Bedi.. and take the pride of our family to great heights like Our Honest police officer Madam Kiran Bedi."

To Roop Lal's comments, there was a great smile on everyone's face, and Ramesh and Subhash echoed. "Yeah, Bhatia *Parivar ki Kiran Bedi banegi, hum sabka naam roshankaregi*[47]"

Usha kept her smile to herself as she observed that Usha ki Kiran now bore the responsibility of enhancing the family's reputation, and she knew deep down in her heart that her daughter would.

****

Poppy seeds danced in the *okhli*[48] As bangles sang of songbirds on the wrists ascending and descending with the pestle. It was a Sunday morning, and Usha was preparing Dodhi for the family. She took some cashews and almonds

---

46 An Indian sweet.

47 She will be a popular personality and will take the pride of her family to great heights.

48 A heavy tool with a rounded end, used for crushing and grinding substances such as spices.

that had been sleeping beside the poppy seeds, submerged them in water overnight, and threw them under the sweet assault of the pestle. A certain feeling of contentment overtook her as she continued to ground the components into a milky consistency. *Dodhi*[49] Works magic for brain health, strengthening memory and vision. This beverage had been passed down for generations along with the feminine urge to drive satisfaction from tending to the family's well-being, and hence, the tradition of preparing and serving it with love was unbreakable as long as concerned mothers, wives, and daughters remained in the family.

Emptying the now grounded contents of the mortar into a cauldron, Usha hummed a tune as she cooked the mixture in ghee. Ramesh was very fond of this recipe as it reminded him of his grandmother, who used to serve it in huge brass glasses, and Usha was always extra careful to prepare it to perfection for her husband. Once the *khaskhas*[50] was browning, she waited for the color to intensify while glancing out into the *veranda* where the three men were sitting together with her daughter. It had been a few months since Kiran had become a part of the family and the little one always kept at least one member of the family on their toes. The child had come to easily recognize every separate individual in her family and had set unique standards of expectations from each. For example, she would start giggling the minute Subhash would go near her, anticipating a new trick to make her laugh.

On the other hand, she had formed a habit of fisting the

---

49 A milk custard made from poppy seeds.
50 Poppy seeds,

collar of her father's shirt and blabbering in baby language to try to communicate with him. Moreover, much to the family's amusement, she would choose to relieve herself during the exact moments Ramesh held her as if trying to get under the skin of her father, who would remain unperturbed, nevertheless. Ironically, the child got along best with her grandfather, who would carry her in his lap, going about his work for hours. During this time with the elderly man, the zestful child would look very calm and contented while she observed her surroundings with wide eyes, without disrupting noises or movements. It was also during this time that Usha, who was always on the qui vive due to the demanding child, received some time to rest.

Finally, Usha added milk into the cauldron, and after a good while of stirring the boiling liquid, she managed to put out the fire in the *angithi*[51] While the custard cooled down, she poured the warm drink into glasses, similar to brass material which resembled the ones Ramesh's grandmother used and carried them outside on a tray.

The three men, who were talking amongst themselves, paused their conversation as Usha put the tray down and reached out for a glass of Dodhi. Roop Lal handed the baby to her mother, who sat down with a tiny katori in hand and started slowly spoon-feeding the custard to Kiran.

"We think it's time to find a sister-in-law for Usha." Roop Lal picked up his glass and took a gulp," Talk to your family and friends, and tell them that the Bhatia's are looking for a wife for their other son."

---

51 A traditional brazier used for space heating and cooking in the northern areas of South Asia.

Usha and Ramesh nodded and looked at Subhash, who, unlike his charming and witty self, was shy and quiet - not meeting the eyes of the couple. This made the family laugh, adding Subhash's bashfulness, " Alright, alright. Stop teasing me." He went inside to finish his drink in peace while the family chuckled after him, accompanied by the baby's giggles.

A month later, Subhash married Kamlesh, making another great addition to the family. The household, which previously consisted of two motherless children with a widowed father, was now a blissful home and a fulfilled family. Soon, Kiran's first birthday was celebrated with much enthusiasm. There had never been such a grand celebration at the Bhatia household, and both the women worked together to clean the house and put-up decorations. The two were living on separate house sections with their significant others and managed their own households during regular days, but both Kamlesh and Usha constantly looked forward to coming together to make special arrangements for festivals and occasions. Making *rangolis*[52] Together during Diwali and pranking their husbands on Holi brought out a friendship between the two, and when it came to Kiran's birthday, the two women weren't going to leave any stone unturned.

"A little to the left," commented Kamlesh as Usha held a party curtain of pink rose petals against the wall.

"Perfect." Usha stepped back and tilted back her neck upwards to confirm this observation whilst still keeping her hands against the wall.

---

52 Traditional Indian decoration and patterns are made with ground rice, particularly during festivals.

"You're right. It's good here. Now hand me the tape." Kamlesh handed the tape to Usha and, once the curtain was in place, helped her step down the chair she had climbed.

"I have tied marigold flower strings around the staircase and *gajar ka halwa.*[53] is ready," announced Kamlesh beaming with excitement. She loved Kiran like her own and could not wait to celebrate the little one's birthday.

"That's wonderful. Let's prepare the snacks, and I will ask Ramesh to take care of the rest of the decorations," said Usha making Kamlesh revert in inquisition.

"But Bhabhi, where are the men anyway?"

Usha took Kamlesh by the elbow and led her quietly towards her room, where the three men sat in a straight line. Kiran sat up on the bed behind them, surrounded by a pillow fort to keep her from falling off, and played with balloons that were being passed to the child every two minutes.

"Are they...?" Kamlesh paused mid-sentence, almost choking with laughter.

"Inflating balloons, yes." Usha let out a muted chuckle while the two sneaked off, trying to remain undetected so as not to interrupt the men's adorable attempt at decoration.

As the two walked towards the kitchen, mimicking the men, laughter tingled in the air as they nudged each other to add one remark after another. While Usha was still lost in the euphoria of the humorous situation, Kamlesh looked at her and said in an edgy tone," Bhabhi, I need to tell you something."

---

53 Carrot Pudding an Indian sweet.

Usha, still smiling, looked at her sister-in-law and realized the seriousness of her tone and expression before mirroring Kamlesh's temperament. Kamlesh had taken a pause, and Usha's face clouded with an alarming concern about what it could be, but she did not think it wise to push.

"I am pregnant."

Upon that, Usha let out a sigh of relief, and her smile and laughter returned," Why are you telling me this good news with a stern face, silly girl?"

Kamlesh let out a smile of her own in return and returned the hug Usha had engulfed her into. Later that afternoon, when the guests had arrived, the good news was broken to the men of the family and to Kiran, who congratulated the mother to be with some blabbering of her own. And so, the birthday of Usha ki Kiran brought another propitious onset.

****

The atmosphere was buoyant and bustling, with celebratory greetings everywhere in the chilly weather of December. Christmas was about to hit, and rows of light were on their way. While the sky was blanketed by thick fog and smoke, there were small fires burning, and it looked like ember lights twinkling like stars. It was as if Santa himself was blowing chilled air towards Delhi so that he could visit Kiran, who was draped in a warm black handwoven sweater. Rubbing her hands together to generate a hint of heat, Kamlesh picked up a soft white shawl and draped it around Kiran as the little girl was blowing warm air on her hands to save herself from the cold. She resembled a little teddy bear that was wrapped under so many layers of clothes. Kamlesh turned towards Kiran, bent down, and came at the same level as Kiran, who was the Centre of attention not only today but every day in the Bhatia household; mimicking the baby voice, she asked little Kiran, "What do you want?" and Kiran made her wonted thinking face, with her finger on her chin and looked up as if mimicking an adult and gave the most childish answer with the brightest smile on her face.

"I want a jalebi."

"No, No, think of something else, something you can play with and dress up," mused Kamlesh.

Now her brain was churning with all the myriad possibilities, and this wheel of chance landed on a doll.

Kiran gave a prompt reply in her baby voice, "I want a doll," and "You will get something just like a doll, guess what?" asked Kamlesh.

Kiran looked up with hopeful twinkling eyes and asked, "A little sister?"

"Yes, you'll soon have a little sister, Kiran. Are you excited?" asked Kamlesh.

All eyes were set on Kiran as she rushed towards Usha and held her little finger, inviting her to dance while she sang her own little song.

"I will play housie with her; then we will jump together, and then we will also play doctor doctor...

Mumma and I'll comb her hair just as you taught me, and then I'll sing a lullaby to her and make her sleep. It will be just perfect."

This sweet little act of hers had caught everyone's attention yet again and received their approbation for her beautiful untainted reflections, and she was completely oblivious, never even having the faintest idea of how her family's attention was going to be shared amongst two.

Out of excitement, Kiran was unwilling to close her eyes for sleep, and Usha had to sing her favorite Lullaby to make her calm down and fall asleep.

One cold morning, the sky was painted azure, and candy-like cotton clouds were floating through the sky as if they were recreating Da Vinci's starry night in the daytime. Kiran was looking at the sky with great wonder in her eyes as if this was the first time, she understood what the clouds were saying to her. She suddenly got distracted and started to call her mother continuously, *"Mumma, Mumma, Mumma."*

Usha was busy making flat breads at the angithi. She started to look around her utensils, searching for something that'll keep Kiran occupied.

It is hard to retain amusement among small children because they get obsessed with things in seconds and forget about them the next, so being born in a comfortable yet not so well-to-do household, often kitchenware or objects of daily use came to Usha's rescue when she or the members were busy in their daily chores.

Her eyes sparkled when they spotted a steel bowl. She waved it towards Kiran, and her lips instantly turned up into a smile as bright as sunshine. Usha then picked up the boat and placed it in a red bucket-filled quarter with water; of course, unaware of objects floating, she became so happy that she instantly started clapping her hands and cooing. Then, she picked up the boat herself, adorned with a sailor cap. She decided that now her boat would float through the whole bucket and make turns. Gently pushing the bowl forward, she started its journey and, along the way, pushed a little too fast; the boat tilted, and water got into the boat, and as a natural reaction, the boat started to sink along with Kiran's hopes. Hit hard by her shattered dreams; she started crying and shouting.

"My bowl is drowning……. my bowl is drowning". Kiran was mumbling these repeatedly until the calamity got noticed by Usha,

Usha turned toward Kiran with an amused expression. Controlling her laughter at that hilarious circumstance, Usha tried to save the boat and brought it up. But to no avail, Kiran was so sad that the fact that the boat was up again didn't console her at all. Despite Usha pacifying Kiran about it, this sharp little girl got so angry that her mother laughed at her mishap. She puffed air into her cheeks and started acting all mad at her mother, only to be laughing the next second when Usha used her age-old weapon 'tickles', the only thing that could make Kiran laugh within seconds but only second to hot piping 'jalebis' which she loved.

Hours turned to days and days to months, the cloudy muggy weather gave way to bright sunshine, and the plant world was thriving in greenery. It was monsoon, the time for rebirth, and the world was all happy again as the earth receives showers and beautiful flowers were making their way into the world of humans. In the Bhatia household, too, fun and frolic were on the way as Kamlesh was due today. She was sitting under the Banyan tree with her hand on her belly and was talking to her little child in a soft voice, "Are you excited to come into this world?" as if trying to answer, the baby started kicking Kamlesh, and soon the kicks turned into labor pains, and she could see her little child's excitement. With a smile on her face, she was rushed to the hospital.

The birds were chirping, and the butterflies were dancing, the newly sprouted leaves of the potted plants in the hospital were flowing as though delighted with the arrival of a little girl whose cries were a melody to her mother's ears. When Usha broke the news to little Kiran, she couldn't stop smiling, and by the time they reached the hospital, her cheeks started to hurt. Nothing could contain her excitement about becoming an older sister. The moment they stepped foot in the hospital, Kiran started running here and there, full of life that she had literally raised the whole hospital over her head, and Usha was struggling to keep up; it was as if sisterhood had given her new jetpacks.

When they finally reached their humble destination, they were greeted with motichoor ke *laddoos*,[54]

but Kiran ignored her second favorite sweet, which usually gave her a profound flip of ecstasy, and ran towards Aunt's bedside. Of course, her little sister was more important than some orange balls of sweet made of ghee that melted the moment it touched your tongue and gave an explosion of taste, spreading happiness to every lip it touched. The moment her eyes fell on the little child, all her excitement instantly turned into warm love; she picked up her finger, being extremely careful

---

54 Crushed pearls balls; an Indian delicacy

with the touch so as not to hurt the child, just looking at a little sister who had given her wisdom beyond her age. She started slowly stroking her forehead, which felt so feeble at every touch. Little Sonu felt connected and instantly gave a smile back. It was as if Kiran's words had touched straight to god's heart, and to her amusement and pleasure, she was exactly like the fluffy doll with grape-like eyes Kiran had imagined.

"Hey, Kiran... hey, big sister..." Subhash hugged Kiran as she entered the room.

"Uncle, the baby is very sweet... she is my little girl... we are going to play together all day long..."

"Of course..." smiled Kamlesh at Kiran

"Now go and eat your favorite delicacy," Usha suggested to Kiran.

It was at this point that Kiran started feeling like an older sister as if she now had someone to look after and take care of, and she did become her whole world of traction before a year later, joined at the hip, and just two years apart it was as if they were cut from the same cloth they used to play *'Ghar Ghar.'* [55] On and at the time 'acting' doctor couldn't separate them even after many unsuccessful attempts at listening to each other's heartbeats that ended with the both of them on their backs laughing like the elephants who had spewed water out of their spouts in their favorite storybooks. To say the least, Usha knew that Kiran had found a true soul companion, but she was blissfully unaware that another was on the way.

---

55 An indoor game.

It was a weirdly chaotic day. Usha had just entered the threshold of the house after providing Ramesh with her handmade lunchbox. She was a little tired today as she had prepared a three-course meal with hopes that it would bring a smile to Ramesh's face, which was a little frazzled with his work these days. When she placed one foot in, little Kiran, with all her angelic charms, came out running to greet her and bought a cold glass of water to provide her with some respite from the heat. The sun was shining a little too bright, and the humidity was creepily annoying everyone while the umbrella and the sunscreen sighed with resignation and deemed themselves a failure. Usha started to feel uneasy and rushed to the bathroom, she started to puke, and later that day, Usha realized that she was pregnant. The Bhatia household went into another fit of frolic; the creases on Ramesh's forehead eased out as another baby was on the way.

They decided to go straight to the Temple to thank God, who had been immensely kind to them, and to take their blessings. The *Prasad*[56] Was the sweet for today, blessed by God himself, just as the baby on the way was.

Holding Usha's hands in the Temple before the idol, Ramesh whispered, "Thank you for fulfilling my life and making it complete." His eyes sparkled with gratitude and love.

"What are you doing...? It's a temple," said Usha in embarrassment, swiftly taking away her hand with a smile. Her coy face made Ramesh's heart brim with an undying love.

"I am just thanking you in front of God." Ramesh smiled

---

56 A devotional offering is made to a god, typically consisting of food that is later shared among the devotees.

and answered Usha. The couple shared the excitement of a newlywed whose honeymoon phase would never extinguish.

You know, Usha... I felt that sky had fallen down when grandma left us. But from the time you have come into my life, there has been not a single day where I have missed my grandma. God has fulfilled my wish to send my lovely grandma in your form back into my life.

I could not be more thankful to God than this!"

Usha smiled with all happiness in the world. After all, what's there to life beyond love?

This time around, Usha got a very positive and nurturing environment and was well cared for by Ramesh, and also by her tangy cravings that arrived unannounced but left her feeling quite content at the end. All her wishes were his commands, and he used to fill her days with all things happy. He always managed to do little things for her that instantly uplifted her mood and energy because it's always the little things that matter the most. One day, she was craving something tangy, and she told Ramesh about it, so he bought a tangy orange candy and presented it to her. She opened the wrapper and popped one into her mouth, delighted. She was slurping away at the candy just when Ramesh presented an orange ice lolly, her face dazzled with happiness, and she took it. She felt so special and loved that she was being pampered, and she felt like a little child once again; this was something splendid that she had never experienced in her childhood; it was as if Ramesh's small gestures made the girl child in her who was lost among all the adult pressures come back to life now that hers was on the way. The orange ice lolly melted in her mouth, and she shared some with Ramesh, too but was quick to finish it because she didn't want all the love to melt away. The love still stays in between these lines, just like Usha's heart-melting smiles and yours. Just as she licked the wooden stick for the last time and was wholly content, Ramesh presented her favorite tamarind toffee covered with sugar. She started jumping like a child, and here on, the love only grew.

Around this time, she was hell-bent on having a normal delivery for her radiant offspring and herself to be in fine feather. She had taken many conscious measures to ensure the same; for starters, she remained super-active and spent her time moving around the house while Kiran kept her on her toes. She could also be seen exercising and eating healthy food, something which is very tough in a Punjabi household. It was around this time that her motherly instincts peaked, and her obvious interest in knitting flourished. It was her daily ritual now; she would wake up, get dressed and go to the local market to buy yarns to make sweaters and very small caps and gloves for Kiran and her future child. The moment she stepped into the house, she would take out the yarn with great desire and sit in her brown wooden rocking chair, with a pillow behind her back, and in a comfortable position would start unwinding the yarn and preparing it to create art. It is impressive that this simple art of weaving a pattern by exquisitely twisting the knitting sticks could tell a lot about a person; the sheer patience and hard work were nothing less than a trophy of love and a warm hug that a mother presented to her child to give them the protection from the chill as well as the cold world.

Immersed in her thoughts, Usha's eyes stuck on the yarn

and two red pencils in Kiran's hands, who was sitting slightly away from her.

Yellow thread of wool yarn was being turned around the two pencils, and the gaze of Kiran was stuck in moving the pencils faster and making the thread clumsier and more stuck between pencils.

"What are you doing, my doll?" asked Usha.

"I am turning the thread between pencils as you do every day", answered Kiran.

"I do every day with Pencils?" asked Usha with raised eyebrows.

"Yeah. You are holding those thin sticks and the thick thread

Like you, I am holding pencils and my thread." Kiran responded in a naïve voice.

"Oh!!! I see.

What are you making?"

"I am making a frock for my doll, Mom."

Usha chuckled upon hearing this and recalled her own mischievous acts when Bala aunty used to do the knitting. Those days still stayed afresh inside her palace of memory, fueling joy and love. How could she even forget the woman who was more like her mother? Though she fell out of touch with her, she always yearned to meet her deep down.

"Mom, my thread is stuck and is not moving ahead. Can you help me?" Kiran's query brought Usha back to reality. Shaking her thoughts off, she quickly went to attend Kiran.

"Oh yes... my dear, why don't you watch my sticks and then

follow for yours?" said Usha to Kiran.

"Mom... But I am going to play with Sonu. Can you make one for my doll too?"

Before Usha could reply, the little girl disappeared into thin air, for she knew her mother wouldn't say no to her.

Usha, along with the doll, was creating a tomato red sweater which was almost done. As she pushed the last yarn in and cut the thread, she felt an immense wave of fractious pleasure crossing her heart. She stood up and picked the sweater up with immediate care because now she could imagine her baby in it. Putting the sweater on her shoulder, she started to tap her imaginary baby and swirled with her around the courtyard while humming her favorite tune, "*lag jaa gale.*[57].

"Who are you hugging, Mom?" Kiran asked her in a higher decibel. Noticing the newly knit sweater, she assumed it was for her. "Is it for me, mom?" She asked Usha with her chin up to catch a look at her mom's face.

"No... dear... this is for your new sibling," said Usha lovingly to Kiran. She patted her cheeks and kissed her. Kiran's blinked at her twice in an attempt to process what she heard.

"Why not for me? I am your princess. Why are you knitting for some other baby?" Kiran's zest and curiosity were now replaced with jealousy.

Usha was taken aback by Kiran's reaction. But, at the same time, she knew this feeling was natural among the elder siblings too. She covered Kiran in a tight embrace and said, "You will soon have another playmate. You will be the big sister, and

---

57 A Hindi song whose translation reads, 'Embrace me.'

the little baby will bring happiness and joy and will play every day with you. You will have him/her by your side always: a true companion."

Little did Usha know that within five minutes, the imaginary baby was going to turn into a real one. Her term was nearly complete, and somehow her happiness had made the little child eager to come out too.

When the pain started and was still bearable, she went out to the street to call a local doula to assist her in childbirth. The kid popped out in no time, and the family got the good news that it was a healthy baby girl, and Kiran was the happiest. It was as if God was showering the Bhatia family to overcome the shortage of females over the last three generations.

A mere string of words couldn't ever do justice to the angelic newborn, but still, we tried; she was, of course, wonderful: her soft milky skin glowed just like her mother's throughout the pregnancy, and her eyes were like pools of honey-sweet just like her smile which was like a rainbow full of colors, her cheeks reddish-pink almost mimicking her mother's blush in her cosmetic drawer and her hair a perfect light brown complimenting her beautiful big eyes looking at people so larger than her with wonder and a twinkling just like the north star.

Holding Baby in his hands, Ramesh uttered, "She is a perfect constellation of the gene pool and a splitting image of her grandfather."

"I am sure she will soon be the apple of his eye," Usha replied with a complacent smile. Usha had always been the leading lady whenever she was. Like every kid, she was submissive during her childhood days. But, as she grew up, she started to have important questions regarding life and society and slowly got the bigger picture of the world she was living in. Gender bias became a huge concern for her while growing up, and it slowly unleashed her rebellious side. Her fearless nature continued to grow, and she wasn't scared to raise her voice and challenge the norms of society. She was going to shine, despite all odds, she would say to herself.

Usha introduced her daughter to the family, and after much deliberation, she was named *Kanchan* because her skin shined like gold. Unlike the Indian tradition of naming the children by a letter picked out by the priest Usha, as the rebel she was, decided to name her children from the same letter 'K.'

After the little child had completed two months, Usha wrapped her in a baby blue sky-like blanket, failing in her desire to carry her offspring in a bunch of fluffy clouds, for it was time to introduce her to the neighbours as she was a mark of pride and as they were eagerly waiting to see the child, they had heard huge praises about. So, she took her to Mrs. Sharma's house, where all the ladies assemble every evening to carry on their usual buzz. The moment their eyes fell on the baby in blue, their eyes smiled in instant recognition, for she was rightly named. Kanchan instantly stole the hearts of all the neighbours, and the songs of her beauty were spread among the knowns. They instantly presented them with envelopes of cash as was the tradition and sang "congratulations" in unison.

"Kiran is three years old, and it's time we think of her education," Usha murmured in a low voice while making the baby sleep. "Did you say something to me?" Ramesh, who couldn't get Usha, asked.

"Oh yes, I was thinking of Kiran's admission to School."

"I know the principal of 'Veenu Teenu Public School.' Let me talk to her about Kiran's admission in the morning."

Owing to her intelligence and inquisitive nature, Kiran was directly admitted to Nursery. Thanks to Usha's homeschooling, it made Kiran ahead of her learning.

Kiran soon gained popularity in the school because of her outstanding handwriting, intelligence, and ardent devotion to studies, unlike other kids. Ramesh and Usha felt very happy and proud of their daughter.

On a Wednesday afternoon, even without changing her uniform: sky-blue shirt and dark blue tunic, Kiran rushed toward Usha with her notebook. She was jumping on her way out of enthusiasm.

"Look, Mom. I got five stars in English." Kiran said while catching her breath. "Not only English, but I also got the same for math too, for writing tables till five. Ma'am applauded me and appreciated all my answers were perfect. She made me stand in front of the class, and the whole class showered me with loud claps."

Usha caught up with changing Kanchan's clothes, didn't turn her head to look at Kiran and gave a plain answer. "I will get back, Kiran. Now change your uniform. You see, I'm busy, right?"

A response like this shattered Kiran's excitement. Her sibling suddenly turned into her rival.

She left with tear-filled eyes to another room and sat until some comfort was offered to her. Nothing happened as per expectation. She went back to the same room to check and saw Ramesh playing with Kanchan, and Usha was busy cooking in the kitchen. Kiran sat stubbornly inside her room without speaking a word to anyone. Before she could remember, she slowly slipped into sleep. After an hour, she woke up to the sound of Usha calling out for her. Usha handed over a tiny, cute cake with a single candle to Kiran and told her it was to celebrate her impeccable academic report. "You will always be our special kid, Kiran. But, you see, Kanchan is so small and fragile, and she has come into this world trusting us. It is our duty to take care of her and give her the best. She is your sister, and she loves you. Her face lights up every time you go near her. She believes in you, in her elder sister. Love her, Kiran, for she loves you too." With these words, Usha handed Kanchan over to Kiran, and Kanchan clutched Kiran's fingers tight. Kiran looked up to smile at Usha. Usha placed her hand above her kids' hands and squeezed them out of love. But, somewhere deep down in her heart, she wasn't convinced and couldn't take all the attention going to Kanchan. Her jealousy subsided, only to erupt again.

Everyone was mesmerized by Kanchan, but Kiran still wanted to be the center of attention, which was a spot she held onto pridefully for three whole years and this new angelic baby girl stealing her spot made her pinkish green with jealousy, and Usha could sense it but before she could have a talk with her Kiran.

On one of the cold chilling mornings, Kiran opened her eyes and searched for her dad; instead, she found Kanchan sleeping on the SPOT where Ramesh sleeps every day. In a fit of rage, she threw little Kanchan, who was sitting on Ramesh's bed, out of the room and huffed and said, "It's my father's bed," and puffed her cheeks up with air and went and sat on the bed huffing and puffing with her arms folded.

Usha and Ramesh acted rather calmly, unlike the normal Indian parents who raise their children by the hand. They decided to talk to Kiran and make her understand that she was wrong.

Ramesh said, "My dear daughter, she's not as big as you are, and she doesn't understand a lot. If you feel you have a problem, you should come and tell us, and we will help you out." and Usha said little Kiran, "Now you're a big sister, and you have to take care of Kanchan" her expressions of pride had now turned into guilt and then realization.

Kiran understood what her parents were trying to tell her and placing her inferiority complex that might swallow her love for the new little baby aside, she decided that now she'll get along with her with unmixed crystal-like emotions. At the same time, her parents informed their co-habitants to pay attention to Kiran as well, as she was feeling left out while they gave both their sweet little girls equal attention and loved them with all their beings.

Kanchan and Kiran were two contrasting personalities prone to clash but had made their peace with each other during the long hours they spent playing together. One fine evening, the cold breeze was whirling around, and it was the perfect time for a game of hide and seek. It was Kiran's turn to find Kanchan, and the clever little Kanchan decided to sit in an almirah so that Kiran could never find her, and she could win the game. But just around that time, Ramesh returned with a kg of hot piping jalebis that Kiran, not even in her dreams, could resist. Before Ramesh could call her out, she moved as if in a trance towards the sweet-smelling box Jalebis took a huge breath in and ran to Ramesh so that she could have it first, while poor Kanchan sat in the almirah for 4 hours and only came out when Kiran had devoured all the jalebis. Just when her eyes saw Kiran slurping and eating the last piece of jalebi, she couldn't help but cry. Her expressions could instantly melt everyone's hearts, but Kiran's satisfactory "wow" saved her from getting scolded that day. They used to play together a lot; they made a game out of wearing dresses of innumerable ranged array and exchanged them and often did a fashion show only reserved for the Bhatia household where Ramesh and Usha sat in the front row cheering for them.

Usha was very cautious of their health and took good care of her children. She used to oil their hair regularly and make them into plaids and force down medicines to strengthen their eyes down their throats while they made squeaky noises and weird faces and ran away. Both Kiran and Kanchan had long, thick, and luscious hair, which Usha used to braid in different styles, and the children loved them. One day, a relative tried to poke Usha saying, "do the girls have lice?" To which Usha slapped back, "No, their mother is still alive."

Usha loved making mud vessels and wanted to pass this art on, which she had acquired from her Bala Aunty. With great delicacy and intricacy, she used to make vases, bowls, and mugs. While teaching this art to her children, she would share with them all her life lessons, tell them funny incidents, and teach them to be fearless women with thick skin but also be sensitive and caring individuals, just as she was the best of both worlds. She used to often tell her children that "humans like clay are made of mud, and it's the strength of our character and our virtues that give us a strong shape which when baked turns into independent individuals," their minds, though mature for their age could never garner the understanding till they turned into mature adults. It was as if while shaping these mud vessels, she was also shaping her children's personalities with great care and perfection with a lot of love, just like Goddess Parvati shaped Ganesh with mud.

One day, the sky was unusually happy, and just after a light morning drizzle, a beautiful rainbow greeted Kiran and Kanchan just before the four of them were going to head out towards the carnival, it was a Wednesday, and on Wednesdays, they wore yellow because that was the only color which was as happy as they were. It was a holiday for Ramesh and a source of pleasure for the other three because it was the only day they could spend together without any hassles and problems. Over the years, Wednesdays became their safe place, so much so that only their own company would set the day straight and make the rest of the week bearable for all of them. Both the girls were jumping and smiling while Usha held onto Kanchan and Ramesh to Kiran, who was on the lookout for a rickshaw that would transport them to the nearby carnival. Kiran and Kanchan sat on their parent's lap while Usha could feel the cold breeze on her face which bought a smile to her lips, her cheeks had a hint of a blush on as it was a happy day, and it caught Ramesh's attention, and his gaze was fixated on her while the children were talking amongst themselves and deciding what to play first. So, when they reached their destination, and the children got down from the rickshaw, they ran towards the carnival, and Usha ran behind them while Ramesh paid the driver. They took the tickets and went in, all hand in hand, towards the large turning wheels where they sat in a cabin, and the wheel started to turn around. Kanchan looked around in awe as it was the first time she had sat on this ride, and with glowing eyes, she looked outside. That's when Ramesh captured the moment in his heart and decided to get the picture clicked from a nearby studio of her little ones, which could be found stuck on the main wall of their house for years and years to come. The moon had started to show since the evening had slowly passed.

"Dad let's go over to the shooting counter next," Kanchan jumped with joy, pointing at the stall with colorful balloons hung on the wall.

"That game looks interesting, Kanchan," Kiran reciprocated with similar enthusiasm and held Ramesh's hand, trying to tug Ramesh in the direction.

"Okay ... okay, kids," Ramesh moved to the stall, succumbing to their innocent and enthusiastic demands. Running towards the stall, Kiran had her eyes on the stuffed Penguin while Kanchan's were on the stuffed Panda.

"Dad, I want that Penguin." Kiran was shouting at the top of her voice to get her dad's attention.

"No, Dad. That Panda looks more beautiful. I want that one, Dad." Kanchan said, grabbing and pulling down the corner of Ramesh's shirt restlessly.

"Penguin.Penguin. Penguin.." Kiran started repeating the same word again and again and started swirling rapidly.

Kanchan said in a broken voice, "Panda. I want Panda. Please, Dad."

Stuck between his girls and unable to choose, he decided that he'd pay for two shots; the rest was all on luck. With great concentration, he tried to look through the small hole over the gun and fixed his eyes on the Panda. After fixing his shot for a whole minute, he went for it. Kanchan and Kiran's hearts skipped a beat, but too much disappointment, the shot touched the shopkeeper's shirt and was nowhere even close to a stuffed toy. Instead of being angry, both girls and Usha started to laugh. With a new decision to prove himself this time, and regardless of all the laughs he heard, he took a leap of faith and went for a shot, and much to everyone's surprise, it had managed to reach the Penguin, with her face mimicking an O, Kiran took the Penguin and started to clap for her father. Her father, as if mimicking a movie scene, turned and flicked his shirt and said, "Now you understand I am not a bad shot. It was just bad luck the first time," and everyone started laughing at him, almost seeing through his little act. Kanchan pulled Usha towards the cotton candy stall as she had already made a pact with Kiran in the rikshaw. It was something she would surely eat today, for it was her utmost attainment of the day. So, Ramesh bought the four of them pink and blue cotton candies, and it wasn't much later that both girls started to fight with the Penguin like little girls do because Kanchan was jealous that she did not get her Panda.

As the curtains of the night began to victoriously conquer

the light of the blue sky, it was time to return home. On their way, they heard a street vendor call out to them, "Chaat Lelo Chaat" (Have Street food). This instantly caught Usha's attention, and she ardently started to look around to search for where she had heard the voice. Her eyes stopped at a middle-aged man wearing a red turban and dhoti with a white shirt, she moved her eyes a little above him and saw the board called "Delhi's famous Chat wala" (Delhi's famous street food), and she started to read further, it said delicious mouthwatering golgappas, a fusion of sweet and savory with a tinge of sourness that instantly burst into your mouth when these fried balls made of semolina flour touch your taste buds. She could instantly feel the golgappa in her mouth, but her stomach's growl broke her trance, and she tugged at Ramesh's shirt and pointed toward the *chaat*.[58] Stall. It sparked his interest, too, and following their line of sight, the children started asking for aloo *tikki*[59]. Now Ramesh had to take them because they were obstinately chanting for chaat. So, they walked towards the chaat stall, and Usha happily gave the order to give us two plates of *Golgappa*[60]" and the vendor handed them two empty bowls, which were filled in second by delicious tangy golgappas. Usha was carefully studying the vendor; he picked up a semolina ball and used his thumb to carve a small hole which he filled with chickpeas and mashed potatoes in a blink of an eye; next, he picked up a spoon and poured it into the sweet and tangy tamarind puree which was the cherry on top of the cake and immersing this amalgamation into a big container filled with tangy water he placed it into Usha's bowl

---

58 Street food.
59 Potato croquette.
60 A type of snack is called water balls.

and when the first one reached her mouth. Her expressions gave a tranquil delight, which could explain the rush of flavors when the golgappa had burst in her mouth. Her first reaction was a little turning up of the nose because of the sourness, and then as the sweetness settled in, it turned into a sigh of delight before they presented their bowl again and asked for another one turned into a sweet smile towards Ramesh who was watching her with great concentration. Both Kiran and Kanchan used to mimic their mother's expressions with great alacrity while she ate the *golgappa*, and Ramesh used to cheer for them. When all four of them were happy and full, they asked for a *Kulfi*[61], so they set out for the Kulfi shop, which was along the way, and there they saw a VCR shop. Both of the girls were fond of movies and would not leave a chance to watch one even if it was in their power. They demanded with great tenacity for it, and Ramesh had to abide by their command, so while going back, they picked up the cassette and rented a VCR and a TV. When they reached home, the whole Bhatia household sat in the courtyard and watched the latest movie, '*Vidhata*'; everyone was impressed with Kunal's character, and Usha was surely smitten.

After the movie, while having rice pudding and sitting comfortably together, Usha asked Kanchan, "Do you want a brother or a sister? And she replied with great conviction, "Sonu Didi has Dheeraj bhaiya as her brother. I want a little Krishna for myself."

---

61 A type of Indian ice cream typically served in the shape of a cone.

Usha replied, "You have a brother already, Kanchan? Dheeraj is your younger brother."

"No, I want my Krishna. Sonu Didi teases me that she has a brother. I want to tease her too."

She rushed towards God's idol and started praying, ":" Oh dear God, please give me a baby brother just like you."

This time Usha and Ramesh were a little anxious about having another girl child and kept their fingers crossed for a baby boy.

It was Autumn, and the leaves were turning orange and rustling down the trees. It was the time for *Navratri*, a Hindu festival that spans over nine nights, and the nine Hindu goddesses were worshipped during this time. It is like the Christian period of Lent, where all indulgences are avoided and is followed by a day called Ashtami, where little girls are worshipped and treated like goddesses and given an offering of *Puri.*[62], halwa, and *chana*[63] called Kanjak. On such a day, Little Kiran and Kanchan were called for Kanjak to a neighbour's house. Little children ran into the house with their lightning baby-like laughter and tickle-tackle of their fully beaded anklets clad in traditional lehenga choli and their signature fish braids. They were served the food and worshipped. An hour later, Kiran went and stood near the holy pyre to earn her blessing, but when she turned, her braid went flying into the diya, and she burnt a part of her hair. The neighbours rushed with water to help her out. In the evening, when they returned to their own home, Usha, and Ramesh, who were very protective and

---

62 Deep-fried wheat bread of India.
63 Chickpeas, especially when roasted and prepared as a snack.

caring parents, were distressed. Following that, Kiran's health became weak day by day, without any concrete reasons, and that made Ramesh and Usha think that their neighbours might've performed black magic on their small girl. This had been the real situation for many a household over there, and Kiran's parents pondered if that could be the case with them too. They paid a visit to their guruji's place to set right things, and everything slowly started to get back to normal. But, deep down, Kiran's parents had a deep-seated will to teach their neighbours a lesson.

A little later, on a Wednesday morning, the sky that day was rather turbulent, and rain had greeted their doors. Usha stood at the doorstep looking at the sky and said to Kiran, "I guess God is weeping today. Remember to take an umbrella before you go out to play," and Kiran replied promptly, "okay, Mumma," but while Kiran was playing outside with her small group of friends it started to drizzle which gave way to a beautiful rainbow, such that Kiran and Kanchan stopped in their tracks to just gawk in awe at the amazing amalgamation of colors which they had often drawn on a canvas from their imaginations, but to view it in real life was a breath-taking experience and to come back and tell it to their mother was another. While the little children narrated their experience, Usha looked so surprised to give the children the joy of explaining the magnanimity of a natural act which was so beautiful, just as their expressions while explaining its different colors. "Mumma, there was violet and yellow and also green! How did these colors reach the sky? Does the god paint the rainbow just as we do in our notebooks?" asked little Kanchan. Usha smiled and explained in great detail the phenomena of a rainbow which was so oblivious to their childish minds that they were so in awe to think that white light was made of seven colors that Kiran kept looking at her white t-shirt and said, "Mumma but this only one color, I have to paint it to make 7". It was then that Usha started to feel slight labor pains and decided to go lie down on her bed. As she was close to the term, she asked Ramesh to call the local doula from the adjacent house. Within minutes of being called, she readily gathered all the necessary equipment and set out with Ramesh for his house. Kiran and Kanchan sensed that something was wrong they followed their mother to the room. They saw her face and instantly held her hand with hopes of easing away the pain. The doula came in the running, assessing the room in her usual fashion and placing her equipment on a tray. She said in a soft voice to Ramesh, "take the girls away from here" Ramesh went and held both of their hands and forcibly dragged them out of the room while, with sad faces, they cried, "Mumma, Mumma." Within an hour they were greeted with the good news "It's a boy," and everyone was so elated that they were at a loss of words and stood huddled outside Usha's room in hopes of catching a glimpse. The usual term 'boy' sounded with an unusual accent for Ramesh, Kiran, and Kanchan, for they gathered up their trembling courage to face the little Krishna of the family. That's when Ramesh opened the door and brought his newborn, for everyone. The moment the grandfather held his little boy in his hands, a sigh of relief left his lips, and he exclaimed, "hare ram," thanking God for such a beautiful baby. All the family members took turns talking with the little child for the first time, and when Kamlesh held him, she silently prayed for another baby boy, too, since she was five months pregnant at that time, and her happiness was evident through the huge smile on her face.

Usha was carefully observing all this from her bed, with a heart filled with contentment, a fatigued body too tired to say something, a little tear filled with joy left the corner of her, and this drizzle soon turned into full and fledged rain. This little one was so filled with joy that he didn't even cry when he was born; he just tried to look around the world with his large eyes and gave random smiles here and there.

The newborn was named *Kunal,* following Usha and Ramesh's desire of keeping the child's name starting with letter K.

Ramesh had run to the neighboring house. In doing so, a blush had crept onto his cheeks, and small drops of sweat greased his forehead; greeting his neighbours, he went on to give the good news to them with the brightest smile on his face "We've been blessed with a baby boy" to which each of them and went onto asking their permission to use their telephone to inform Daya Ram about the birth of their third child, he rushed to the telephone hastily and "Namaste Papa, we've been blessed with a baby boy. We hope you can come to bless him too soon" to which Daya Ram exuberantly replied "I wish everyone remains happy and healthy and may this little Krishna bring lots of prosperity to you and your family, he told him that they were busy that day and will try to visit them soon," but this was his small attempt at mischief and to surprise them when he reached their house around 8 pm with a box of sweets and good wishes that radiated from his happy disposition. His first step into the house instantly brought the whole family to their feet, and they rushed to hug and congratulate him on becoming a grandfather for the third time, and each time he was happier than the last. The birth of a boy had made his spirits waltz to a symphony. He felt a pleasure within him that ravished through every single cell in his body. He couldn't contain his excitement anymore and followed Ramesh towards Usha's room, where Usha was playing with little Kunal and kept repeating 'Mumma' as if he would spell his first words on that day only. Usha was dead serious that she would win the contest Ramesh had challenged her to; the last two times, a sigh of victory had escaped her lips when both her daughters naturally spoke "Mumma" first, one strike more and she would be named the reigning champion, and she would rejoice in her air of victory and tease Ramesh for years to come. On noticing her father cross the threshold, she lifted her face to give a small blissful smile, and calling her father towards him, she asked for his blessings. "Papa, we have named him Kunal; he will make us shine." Happiness that had resided began to flow as mild waves with a feeling of warm love in his heart for the past three hours manifested itself through the small morsels of tears that were flowing through Dayaram's eyes. He finally rejoiced that her daughter's family was complete and was satisfied that she had given birth to a male child. While these thoughts crossed through his mind and escaped as silent prayers to the kind god, a small phrase escaped his lips "Long live, my child!" The phrase holds its own depth.

Ramesh, in his thoughts, recalled how a family consisting of only three men was now blessed with three kids of him and two of his elder brother Subhash (Sonu and Dheeraj), and a third was on its way. How will I be able to manage the expenses of three kids? The school fee of an English medium school is very high.

I need to give less of my stock on credits. The incessant chain of thoughts to handle the upcoming responsibility hurtled in his mind to the point where he felt restless. Ramesh ruminated deeply about how he was going to manage everything. Then, he calculated every aspect inside his mind and drafted several pre-plans to run things smoothly.

The Birth of Kunal was followed by the birth of Subhash and Kamlesh's daughter, Rama, just four months apart. Kunal filled their lives with joy and prosperity, and their family was finally complete by the traditional notion of obtaining both male and female children now. Roop Lal was elated as finally, the family of both his kids, Ramesh and Subhash, would flourish, and Kunal and Dheeraj would carry on the lineage. You could almost feel contentment radiating through his voice when he spoke, "after so many years I have experienced this feeling, a complete family in our lineage was a rarity until now, I hope they carry forward the respect of our family and take us forward with their humble and amiable dispositions" exclaimed Roop Lal sitting in a comfortable circle surrounded by his family in his courtyard later that day.

Ramesh's business flourished after Kunal's arrival; the tailoring material, which was earlier a delivery from door to door to tailor shops, converted into a full-fledged business. Ramesh started a new business, he took a humble shop in the "Shiv Nagar" market, where the board was painted red, and the white letters with a black border read 'KUNAL TAILORING MATERIAL.' The shop had two entrances, greeted with a glass door; you'd step into a shop with various suiting materials and materials for blouses on display like a Pantone of colors waiting to embrace your soul and instantly bring a smile to your face, on a corner you could see carefully carved buttons, hooks and dupattas waiting for a customer to make them theirs. Their shop was as full of colors as their lives, and Kunal had only made everything better.

It was Wednesday, which was home to their little ritual; Ramesh's holiday was the perfect excuse for the little children to meet their grandfather. The moment the children returned from school, they would run into the house and, at warp speed, would change their clothes, and after chugging in the food, they came running to Ramesh. Adjusting her clothes, Kanchan asked Ramesh, "*Papa.*[64] Should we go?" to which Usha would shout from her small dressing table, "hey, wait for me, don't rush," and in a minute, she arrived dressed in a beautiful golden Zari blue saree, looking like a goddess and her three children looked at her with awe, while Ramesh couldn't keep his eyes off her. They collected some fruits and set off for Paharganj so that Usha could meet her parents and siblings. They went out and got seated on their chetak scooter, Kanchan sat between her parents while Kiran stood at the front, and Usha held Kunal, halfway through both of them started humming to a song that matched perfectly to the vibe of the day, and the trees were dancing under a soft blue pleasant sky, cool winds gave respite from the smoldering heat characteristic to Delhi, it was unusually pleasant, like the day that would be perfect for a trip to India Gate, the favorite picnic spot for Delhiites with lush green lawns and a view that instill pride in the hearts of every Indian.

---

64 One's father.

When they reached their destination, the anxious kids weary of the journey ran in search of their favorite orange drink Rasna. They ran in, calling out to their grandfather, "Naanu, Naanu," greeted him, and went straight to the kitchen to cool down. Usha entered, flustered with so much to hold and no space for Kunal, so she hastily handed him over to Ramesh with the utmost delicacy, who was placing his scooter on the stand. Daya Ram waited for her dear Usha on the threshold of the house, hugged and gave her blessings. Then Daya Ram instantly rushed to the kitchen to find his little friends whom he waited earnestly for every Wednesday and hoped that they would stay longer by the time the day came to an end. So, while handing them bottles of cold water to pour into the Rasna concentrate, he would steal a glass for himself, even though strictly advised not to by the doctor, and reminisced how he would chug a large glass of Rasna when he returned after playing cricket with his colony friends in his days. When the kids were settled and happy, he would introduce the idea of going for a walk to the local market, all of them held hands, and Dayaram, with his stick and his signature turban, would walk in complete pleasure while these children shared their little stories with him.

On the way, he would often stop by a street vendor for something that would bring a tinge of savory to their taste palettes, like tamarind or *amrakh*[65] He was fond of munching on such stuff and would often rush to his door when such costermongers would visit their lane and made sure to save some orange candies for his little friends. While they enjoyed

---

65 A tangy star fruit

these delicacies, Dayaram would often steal a bite from each one of them, and when the kids threatened or teased him, he would buy them chocolates and take little pinky promises from them to keep it a secret from Usha. It seemed as if he was living his childhood again vicariously through these little bundles of mischief. He loved the children wholeheartedly so much that it would be visible through his eyes and the way he talked to them. He was the best grandfather one could ever ask for.

Kunal was a playful young entity whose favorite pastime was to play with water; he would scoop it up in little palms full and watch it trickle down his fingers, Usha watching from a distance used to muse as to how people are like water, too, quick to fit in and change forms according to their circumstance, a considerable high in their lives had provided them with the luxury of television which was a far cry a little while back, but her insight of the human nature helped her never fill up with pride even though they were considered well to do, she remained humble and made sure her family stayed grounded too.

Ramesh was very fond of roses and grew them in various colors in their terrace garden. Red, pink, yellow, and white, just like the colorful shop, he wanted to fill his house with all the colors too. Each morning he gifted a fully bloomed rose to Usha, the everlasting rose of her life, which was quick to give a pink sheen to her cheeks and a smile she tried so hard to hide when she reached the kitchen, Kamlesh used to say, "Ohh you got a rose again today???" and she used to glance at her and start to laugh and in a soft tone replied, "stop teasing me, Kamlesh, focus on the food."

Soon they brought home their television. Well, after Kiran, the television became the center of attraction; every Sunday, the children had a packed schedule; they would sit in front of the tv at 9 am and watch Ramayana and Mahabharata, which were religious shows that aired every weekend on Doordarshan. After two hours of constant entertainment, they went to study, then they had to play in the evening and came back to a movie that aired around 8 pm. All in all, their Sundays were quite eventful. Occasionally, they would watch *Vikram Betaal* and *Chitrahaar* together too. The kids were having a good time; around this time, they had renovated their house and made it into a three-storied humble abode which the kids used to love because it gave them ample space to play hide and seek. Usha was also happy as her family was thriving, and she had no scope to complain. Now that their family was comfortable, she started saving for the children's wellbeing and education so that they could ensure for them a good and prosperous life. Everything was going well until Ramesh started to face financial instability in his business. As most of the material from his shop was taken on credit by Tailors

Chapter
5
Price of Duty

Chapter 5
Price of Duty

Ramesh's reaction to these sudden losses was rather inspirational: he stood back up and used his savings to run his household. He bought some more materials to sell in the shop. But the stress of keeping it all together, handling the responsibilities of his family, paying for the education of his children, and a lack of strong capital had started to bring back the creases on his forehead and dampened his spirits. He would spend his evenings with his constant companion 'stress' and tried his level best to keep smiling even when he was with his family, trying to protect them from these hassles as he just wanted to keep them happy. Whatever it took to safeguard his family from the impending misery, he skillfully did it all. But his battle within himself started to suck him off all the life that there was, and his condition only began to grow worse. His carefully carved silence roared in the known presence of Usha, unlike the minced words that echo through a jarring anxious mind waiting for the interaction to be over before it even started. It was as if he wanted Usha to understand his silence, and she did. The secrecy, the anxiety, and the uncertainty of the future made him avert his eye when Usha demanded contact. He started to arrive late to the house and was scared to face the family members lest they ask the cause for his behavior. Unaware of what was happening to her family, Usha carried on tending to her duties and her children. Though she started to observe Ramesh's erratic behavior, she underestimated the extent of financial instability they were in and hoped for a better time.

Around this time, Dayaram fell sick. His habit of stealing a savory bit here and there had been proven detrimental to his health. Nishok and Anku took him to a doctor who advised him to be admitted to the hospital. They informed all their sisters, who were well settled in their own households after marriage, about their father's condition. Such bad news had agitated them, and they came as soon as possible to meet their father, except for Usha, who was oblivious to what was happening around her.

Usha and Ramesh did not have a telephone, and all messages were relayed to them by their neighbours, and this news got lost among the countless phone calls they received that day. Nishok was worried about Usha as she did not revert, and he tried the next day again to relay the news somehow to them. It was then that the neighbours informed Ramesh about Daya Ram. The moment this news reached his ears, he was filled with sudden pangs of anxiety and was guilty that the delay was because of him.

Ramesh entered the home with an exhausted face.

"Where were you all the time? I am making your favorite potato curry for dinner. Remember how you would keep on nagging me for it? So today, I am making it without you asking," said Usha holding her ladle like a trophy. Her face was glowing with a full smile.

"Hmmm. I'm not hungry anyway." Ramesh replied in a disinterested voice and left the place.

"You've been not eating these days properly. What's wrong with you?" Usha replied in a concerned voice.

Ramesh grabbed Usha's shoulders and gave her one stern look before saying, "I want to tell you something," Ramesh said.

"I understand you have been worried due to the credit to tailors."

"Did Ramlal tailor not pay today? You went to meet him, right?"

"Yeah... he didn't pay."

Perplexed in his thoughts, Ramesh was figuring out how to break the news to Usha. Finally, with a confused disposition, he just spoke loudly, "Usha, your dad is unwell and hospitalized. Nishok bhaiya called. They made several calls yesterday so that you can come and meet him. However, our neighbours were busy delivering the message." He blurted out everything as his nervousness was pumping inside him insanely.

The spatula fell from her hand, and her expression became blank. She was seized by sudden shock and fear. The spatula fell in the most dramatic fashion leaving its mark all across the floor, and Ramesh was tracing its trajectory as he couldn't bear to look into Usha's eyes as he blamed his incapacity not having a telephone for such a delay. However, he could feel her emotions reverberating through her tear-stained red eyes and instantly felt the love she had for her father.

They rushed to the hospital that day in haste, and Usha had packed some food for Nishok and Anku, who would stay the whole night with her father. On reaching there, she fearfully entered the room and saw her father hooked to machines, and her eyes widened with shock. His condition was much worse than she had expected. Collecting herself, she searched Nishok's face for an updation and asked, "What does the doctor say?" to which he replied softly, "He's doing better than yesterday. Though there's hope, he doesn't have much to say." Hoping for everything to get better, she sat there on a chair in front of her father and started talking to him, even though he was resting. It was her small way of showing concern, something that she had inherited from her mother. She used to often talk to herself, which was her way of venting out. "I knew it. You were always ready to go against the doctor's advice. Kanchan once came and told me that you ate tamarind with them, but I let it go because I thought it was a one-time thing; I should've scolded you, then you would've been better" after spewing a few more sentences in reproach, she couldn't hold back her tears that were already flowing out. Nishok came closer to the chair and started rubbing her back in a circular motion and consoled her that "He'll get better, don't worry", and hugged her, while Ramesh, after checking up on Dayaram, had gone to search for the doctor and talk to him. When he returned, Usha decided it was time to go home. She was relieved that he'll get better and made a mental note to check up on him every hour. That day was filled with turmoil for Usha; she couldn't sleep and only changed sides the whole night. Meanwhile, Ramesh tried to be her rock, and though he tried to empathize, he couldn't really understand what she felt.

Ramesh, who was very upset the day before, had gone to the local telephone office to apply for a telephone connection to get a telephone to avoid such delays in the future, and it became a necessity in case of an emergency. He paid a lump sum fee to get it. The telephone was one of the limited luxuries of those days. In addition to the tailoring material business, the business of public telephone was now set up. It was Usha's ardent wish to avoid such a delay for anyone in the future, and she wanted to heartily help those in need, so she let them give their telephone number to their families to contact. It also started to act as a secondary income; it got them a revenue of 3 rupees for a 3-minute call.

Since Usha made up her mind to do hourly checks on Dayaram, she called Nishok from time to time to check on him and also ensured that food reached him at the right time. She would often go to check up and talk to the nurse to take good care of her father. Meanwhile, Ramesh tried hard to support her in whichever way he could whether it was to crack funny jokes to ease her mind or console her when her mind was clouded with sheer stress.

The whole family that night was having dinner together at the dining table. Usha and Kamlesh had prepared *dal chawal*[66] And all of them were sitting together. Usha was lost in her own train of thoughts and slowly chewed morsels of food. Ramesh, who noticed all this from the corner of his eyes, felt helpless because this time, he couldn't make her problems vanish, and it was really painful for him to see her like that. The phone rang in its usual baritone, wiping away Ramesh's thoughts in an instant. Ramesh stood up and went to answer the phone. "Dayaram is no more" the moment these words had reached his ears, the whole world stood still for a moment, and every

---

66 Rice and lentils.

sound around him narrowed down into a dull, monotonous syllable. His mind had started usual processing thinking of Usha. He called her subconsciously and handed her the phone with his limited understanding of the situation. He knew that he couldn't even imagine uttering these words to Usha, but she ought to know. Within seconds of placing the receiver on her ear, the receiver was on the floor, and Usha had fallen to her feet while she tried to understand the seriousness of the reality which had hit her like an avalanche.

An ocean of tears started flowing, and the fall of Usha made everyone in the house gather around her.

"What happened, Usha?" Kamlesh asked in a panic state.

"Ramesh. What happened?" Kamlesh directed the question toward Ramesh.

"Her Dad is no more," Ramesh uttered in sheer sadness.

Kamlesh hugged Usha tight and also started to cry, "I told you to go and stay with him for a few days. I would have taken care of kids and Ramesh." Kamlesh rubbed gently on Usha's back, who was crying inconsolably.

Just an hour ago, she had called Nishok, and he had informed her with great conviction that everything was well, so she was filled with disbelief, and she constantly battled with denial. She couldn't convince her mind that something like this could happen. After her self-denial took off her, she gave a stale look at Ramesh with great pain and spelt "let's go" strugglingly.

Meanwhile, Kamlesh prepared her bag with the required clothes that they would need to change into after the cremation of the body.

Ramesh understood what Usha meant and tried to control himself from falling apart because he had to be Usha's rock; at least, that's what he thought. So, they had set off for the hospital on their scooter. The journey towards the room was a strenuous one; she was tired, angry and not a speck in her body could accept that her father, the one person whom she loved more than Ramesh, who had made sure that her daughter remained comfortable despite the circumstances, was no more. To Usha, it looked like the world had come to an end after losing her father. The moment she entered the room, her eyes fell on the lifeless corpse. It struck her as a nightmare, petrifying her in open daylight, sucking out all the air from her lungs. She let herself fall apart, and Ramesh held her, controlling his own silent tears.

The grief slowly spread through her body like cracks through freshly thawed ice. She could feel her heart hurt, and this hurt was not like heartbreak; it was as if someone had torn through her skin and snatched her heart out slowly, painfully, torturing her to feel their every move without even flinching or batting an eyelash. Her bloodshot eyes spoke another tale of betrayal. Within a matter of minutes, she became an orphan, and the world stopped or as if the earth had opened through, and she was asking God, "What should I do now? And God remained speechless. Though she was caught in this beef with God, all of this was happening in a small corner of her mind. On the hospital floor, looking at his wife wailing, Ramesh could hear his heart shatter into tiny little pieces, but the only words that left his shuddering lips were, "I'm here for you, and I'll always stay." That little, tiny word "always" was the only respite because now 'stay' seemed transient and life ephemeral. He kept chanting the same words hoping it would reach and mend her broken parts. In fact, words were like band-aids, but the wound was too deep to cure; it was only Ramesh who kept reminding her that she was strong because the voice in her head had already decided that she couldn't take this anymore.

After hours of standing there as a shield, Ramesh decided to pick her up and take her to Nishok's home, wherein the lifeless body was to be brought in for the last Rituals. He talked to Nishok, offered them help, and took Usha home.

There lay the lifeless body of Dayaram on the floor. Hardly before two days, he was sitting on the rocking chair and eating his favorite savories.

No one could imagine a strong man like him was no more; free from his worldly responsibilities and has gone to meet her Padvamati above the clouds.

Usha and her siblings were uncontrollable. They could never imagine in their worst dreams that their father to be no more.

Soon, the body was given a bath by Nishok and Anku and was made ready to be taken for their final journey to the cremation ground.

And the journey started, Dayaram's body was kept on the wooden surface, which was lifted by four men, and there was Nishok moving ahead of the body with everyone around them chanting.

"Ram Naam Satya Hai[67]"

As per Hindu customs, women are not permitted to be on the cremation ground, and they stay back. Usha, along with

---

67 God's name is supreme.

her sisters and Anita Bhabhi, stayed back to clean the house.

It would be an exaggeration to say that she 'tried' to sleep that night after her dad's body was transitioned into ashes, but after looking at her children, it did hurt a little less.

Days passed in a blur, her hands moved, but her whole body stayed blank. Whenever someone tried to talk to her, she would unknowingly give an absent-minded reply. But she tried her best to stay present with her children because their smiles and their talks in some way healed her aching heart. Slowly and steadily, time did work its magic, and though her lively spirit was not restored fully, she felt better, and her family could feel the progress. They were very supportive and joined hands to help her in healing. It wasn't easy, but time filled up the gaps and the cracks as acceptance started to sink in, and she started to feel strong yet again. Slowly she understood that this was her family, and she had to be their rock. It dawned on her that nostalgia was deceptive. So, one day she decided to let it go, she got more involved with her children, tried to cater to all their needs, and helped Ramesh with his shop, and soon the wounds started to heal, even though the scars shall remain there forever.

She became the love she searched for all her life in her father, and that's how she healed by pouring over the love she was supposed to feel.

Slowly, as life came back to normal, her focus shifted towards Ramesh and their business as she was mindful of there being some minor problems. She started to get involved with Ramesh, who was happy because he thought it would help divert her mind. She would often go to the shop in the afternoon and would stay there for 3-4 hours and come back home at night with Ramesh. He appreciated the extra hand, and Usha felt gratified by her involvement. Within days, she had become friends with most of their regular customers, and in addition to Ramesh's goodwill in the neighborhood, Usha's warm, cordial home-like atmosphere brought their customers back, knocking yet again on their doorstep, because of which their shop did well unlike others of the same line of business. They were kind and loving and would derive great pleasure from helping others and lending a hand to the less fortunate. It was this need to do better for a society which made them trust and give tailoring material on credit, but this kindness soon became their enemy.

Ramesh saw his hard-earned money turn to dust, with no visible funds in hand, and soon the stress soon took a toll on his health. One day, he was sitting in his shop and counting some cash. The moment he found out it was not enough to last even a month; he started to hyperventilate and worry about how they will manage their household. He was taken to the hospital as he fell unconscious. Upon arrival, it was ascertained that he had suffered from a heart stroke. The whole family rushed to the spot, and Usha couldn't control her tears; she felt as if her whole world was turned upside down. She repeated the phrase, "Toughen up, you're a strong woman," and after maintaining her composure, she went to talk to the doctor, who told her that it was due to excessive stress. It broke her heart, but she knew that it was her turn now to be their rock. That's when Usha made a firm decision that she'll step forward and be the man of the house so that her husband could rest and recuperate. Upon his discharge, the doctor strongly recommended not to take stress as it would deteriorate his health further.

They started once again to build their lives up from scratch. Usha started to work for the alteration of clothes at her house to run her household and earned some extra income by knitting sweaters. Her priorities were always straight: to give a good life to her children and ensure that her husband's health improved. She took everything in her hands, from managing lenders who gave them money to recharge their shop's stock to the tailors who disappeared with no intention to pay back. Simultaneously, the children were growing up, and Usha had to ensure that their financial situation would have no impact on her children. She moved mountains to shield them from any problems and stress that prevailed in the household. Unable to balance the debts, Usha decided to sell the house, the one which she had built with love and care herself. It was a tough decision but a necessary one to ensure the well-being of her family.

So, she talked to a local broker about selling the house and the shop. Mr. Sharma was very sympathetic towards their situation and tried to talk them out of it. He said, "Sister, what will you do after you sell the house? Don't take a decision in haste; sit on it and decide. I'm aware that things have not been in your favor; could you consider taking a loan?" But Usha was dead serious. "I am certain, Mr. Sharma, it's a vicious cycle; taking a loan would do more harm than good. My children are growing up, and I can't bear to be stuck in these shackles. I want them to open their wings and fly, not to chop them off before they even have a chance. Anyways, it would be peaceful to live in a smaller house than here. Please look for a buyer as soon as possible, *Namaste,*[68]" to which Mr. Sharma replied affirmatively and left convinced.

The next day, at 9 am, Mr. Sharma called and informed Usha about a prospective buyer, The Singhs, a family of six. Usha elatedly informed Mr. Sharma that he could bring them by. The moment they entered the house, they bought a whiff of cheer, as was their disposition, filling the house with laughter and chuckles. The idea of having such a large house and having rooms to themselves attracted the youngest daughter, and her eyes instantly sparkled when she looked at a room that was a perfect manifestation of her mood board, and she sighed triumphantly and exclaimed, "I have decided this will be my room!". Usha was a silent spectator; though her heart ached to see a house that she had designed with such warmth and built with her own two hands being somebody else's home, she was also happy that now they could live without the constant looming threat of all this turning to dust in a matter of seconds owing to their financial instability. She stood with her back to the door frame, drowning in deep thought, when Mr. Singh looked at her and said, "Usha ji please show us the kitchen" Turning towards him with a soft smile, she directed them to the place she spent most of her time in. The kitchen was huge, and that caught Mrs. Singh's eyes, but her eyes instantly diverted to one small nook: the small corner balcony attached to the kitchen

became Usha's sanctuary when the house was too loud for her mind or when she wanted to be alone for a few minutes, but now she'll no longer have such a space, and she wondered how would she ease her mind at the back of her mind. Mrs.

---

68 Greetings to you.

Singh was as impressed as Usha when she stepped foot into the Bhatia house for the first time. She wondered how it had changed significantly since then, and it was their love and hard work which transformed this into their sweet little home. She placed her hand on the wall around which Kanchan and Kiran often played. She could feel all those pencil indentations that adorned the wall, the small height marks which she had made of her children; when she waved her hand over it, she instantly got transported to her happy, laughing, jumping kids who were fighting "I'm taller" "No, Kanchan, I'm older so I'll be taller" and she just wanted them to remain that way forever. She reminded herself that it was for their well-being that she was selling this house.

Another summons from Mr. Singh brought her out of her reminiscent trance; they said to her, "Usha ji, Thank you for the walk-through. I will go back and discuss it with my family. Meanwhile, please let us know what your demand is for the house."

"Thank you, Mr. Singh, for your visit. I have shared my ask with Mr. Sharma."

"Sure, Usha ji. I'll have a chat with Mr. Singh," responded Mr. Sharma as he witnessed the dialogues between Usha and Mr. Singh.

The phone rang the next day, and Kunal answered.

"Who is this?" Kunal spoke in his childish voice

"Kunal, beta. This is Sharma, Uncle. Please hand over the phone to your mother," said Mr. Sharma from the other side of the receiver.

"Mumma... Sharma uncle wants to talk to you." Kunal pulled Usha from the kitchen.

Usha answered, and Mr. Sharma informed her that Mr. Singh had agreed to purchase the house but that they were under a limited budget and would wish to purchase at 10% less than the quoted price."

Usha thought for a second and realized the factor of time was more important. The sooner she gets rid of loans and debts, the better it will be for the kid's and Ramesh's health.

"We have a deal," Usha responded and was very happy that finally, they'll be free. The deal materialized in a few days. She had enough money to pay the lenders and some extra in hand too.

She started to look for a humble house. Her siblings advised her to buy a home rather than pay monthly rent, which would be an added hassle. Soon, the search for the house began on a limited budget. Ramesh and Usha would get up every day and set out at 9 with a broker to help them look for a home. After several weeks of search, they finally found a newly constructed house that fit their budget. The name of the colony was "Kiran Garden". She was filled with pleasant disbelief when she listened to that for the first time. Usha was emotional and felt a signal from the Universe that this would be the place wherein she would be living for the rest of her life.

Usha smiled at Ramesh with an enlightened expression and exclaimed, "this shall be my last!"

Ramesh held Usha's hand in reassurance with a look of contentment and uttered, "same with me," in a very reflective and firm tone. These words at the moment meant eternity to them. When relationships go through ups and downs, they become stronger and evolve an unconventional mutual understanding. Unfortunately, Usha and Ramesh were going through the worse. But they didn't let their external situations change their hearts and love and respect for one another. Instead, they grew only closer.

"Seems like we just met yesterday...." Ramesh's eyes were wet by then and all treasured and highlighted moments of their life peaked into Ramesh's memory lane as a series of meaningful photographs; the images that he holds closest to his very own being

"How swiftly time carries us from one role to another! We are now the parents of three. So, our dreams regarding our kids should be considered seriously. We are their parents. It is our responsibility." Usha replied, choking on the saliva in her mouth.

"I promise you, Usha... This is where we'll raise our kids and upheave their status and societal position.".

"Yes, my darling husband, I have faith in you. A strange thought entered my mind when I got in here. This is it: This shall be, the place where every duty is going to be met and my cradle when I'm no more. Hands down! I settle for this. There's absolutely no other better place for us than this." Usha said in a determined voice and fixed her look on the bird enjoying her flight in the vast blue sky.

"You echoed my sentiments. This is where I want to let out my last breath." Ramesh smiled as he joined Usha in enjoying the view of the bird.

"Ah! We, sentimental geeks! Let us not mention this again. It's going to be a wonderful life, after all." The bird was now gone, and they both turned toward each other and sighed with a half-born smile. Soon, they decided to look at the house because all prior information was from hearsay. The moment they stepped into the colony; the pleasant atmosphere eased their blurred faces. They instantly felt connected to the territory, not just by its name. Usha looked around and asked her children, "Look how green this place looks! Do you like it, Kanchan?" Kanchan gave a vague response and commented her own house was better. Moving forward, Ramesh pointed toward a few children and told them, "Look, the kids here seem to have a lot of fun. maybe you can make them your friends, will you, Kiran?" Kiran replied in a bemused tone, "Maybe, but I like Bavi more; she's my best friend".

They followed Mr. Sharma into the house. On a first look, the house, though small, seemed welcoming. The home wasn't lavish like her previous three-storied building, but it was a modest two-room house. Usha liked it, and upon assessing the living situation with great critical detail, she decided that this would be a good investment. Usha was happy because now the future would be better, and they no longer will have sleepless nights and stressful days, and from here on, peace will be the one thing that shall stay. But the kids who got accustomed to their last home, which was relatively large with three washrooms, found it hard to get along with the present one that had only one restroom. There used to be silly fights every day on who got to use it first. Besides, leaving behind their old friends caused their hearts to grieve silently, and they were worried about how the new kids over there would receive them. Mostly, these were the thoughts of Kiran and Kanchan. Kunal was too small to worry about all these things.

They paid the leftover funds and prepared to move as soon as possible. Ramesh registered the property in Usha's name, who was the lady luck of his life and to whom he owed his life.

Winters had arrived, bringing with it its characteristic gusty winds and thick haze. Kiran and Kanchan had just celebrated their last birthday in their house, but now it was time to move. Usha and Ramesh were busy packing the stuff into boxes while the kids roamed around, making a bigger mess than what was already there. They were unaware of the reason for the house shifting, but their minds were filled with excitement as they thought about the possibilities. Kunal used to ask Usha again and again, and she would reply that "We are going to a new place because I know you were bored with your old friends and used to fight a lot with them, so we wanted you to have new friends and are moving to a better colony." But then all of them formed a troop and started revolting against it, saying they loved their old house, friends, and toys and were apprehensive about moving. Kiran was the older one, and her brain was running at an immense speed trying to figure out the reason, but out of the hundreds of myopic possibilities, the real reason was too far-sighted for her tiny brain. So, with hopes, Kanchan came to Kiran to look for some answers; Kanchan asked, "Didi, will we ever be able to play with Bavi, Puneeta, and Runa?". Kiran wondered with a heavy heart, and without disclosing her real feelings, she tried to cheer up Kanchan by saying, "Don't worry, I've heard that there are more kids who are absolute fun over there. We will make new friends". Soon the packing was over, and they had to vacate the house,

The soul of the space was lovingly crafted over time when Usha entered after her wedding. The memories they made there, bit by bit, laugh by laugh, with some heartache thrown in for good measure, make it seem inconceivable to ever leave the house after selling. We say that it's the memories and people that make a home, not the things in it or the structure itself, yet when we're forced to leave a treasured home behind, it doesn't merely tug at the heartstrings — it damn severs them.

As Usha watched the movers load the last boxes onto the moving truck, she felt like her heart was carrying the load instead of the truck. Her burden seemed to pull her into a vortex of never-ending nausea. Ramesh knew that their pain was overwhelming. In a consoling tone, Ramesh whispered into Usha's ears," We've all discovered now that it's possible to grieve the passing of a home, too. So, let's move and build our new house. Our new home wherein we live without any stress and raise the kids into who we wanted them to be."

Usha nodded in agreement.

The house at "Kiran Garden" had a unique environment and was pleasantly different from their previous household. Here the trees and the surrounding greenery were abundant, and nature was more significant than the artifice. Living in such an environment was not only therapeutic. It also worked in their favor as the children who were so heartbroken after the goodbyes started to enjoy the pleasures of living close to nature. Kunal and Kanchan were excited to spot new birds and flowers and would get up with a jetpack of excitement to go for a walk in the pavilions of nature. So, when the three of them ventured out each morning, apart from wandering around, they came across a park with many swings. There they found many children playing. After looking around and ascertaining that they were all of their age group, they decided to go forward and talk to a little girl who looked like them and had two pigtails. Kiran, their older and much of a public speaker, introduced herself and her siblings. The little girl said that her name was Ruby and the children around her were her siblings: Kannu and Sonu. Everyone introduced themselves with great ardor and coerced them to play a game of hopscotch.

So, Kiran went and looked around for chalk and, after finding one, made the boxes, and Ruby filled in the numbers. Each of them stood on a line jumping with one leg; they finished a whole round. Kiran won while Kanchan lost. Ruby, Kannu, and Sonu won all three games. They decided to see each other again simultaneously and returned home because their parents would be worried. They similarly met each day and became close friends. On some days, Kannu brought her bicycle, and they would all take turns riding it around the colony. This interested Kunal more than anyone, especially those who would ask Kannu for her bike daily.

"Kanu, Can I take the bicycle for a ride?" He would talk in a voice that makes anyone say yes. Kannu used to extend the key to Kunal every time he asked for a ride and would say, "Take it, Kunal. Have a good time." Kunal would fly in the cycle as if he had conquered the entire world inside his fist.

Meanwhile, at home, Ramesh had started to feel better, and the change was working wonders with his health. It made him stand up again with a desire to restart his business and support his family. So, he would enthusiastically wake up every day and start selling tailoring material by visiting a tailor shop. He rekindled his old connections and coerced them to buy the tailoring material from him. He also made new customers around Kiran Garden. Usha was elated on seeing her husband's good health but at the same time worried that in the foresight, she knew these funds wouldn't be enough to suffice as the children were growing up, and so were their needs and demands. Hence, she started to knit sweaters on demand for different customers. She started spreading this news among her new colony friends, who gave her small orders. Word of mouth travelled around vouching for her quality of work, and she got plenty of orders before the beginning of winter that year.

However, naturally, she had no work during the summers. So, she started altering and repairing clothes, making minor adjustments according to the customers' wants.

"Arey, Usha, you are charging too much! I can only give you 20 for this," a customer yelled, standing at her door. Pooja made up her mind already to not give even a paise more than 20 and was ready to defend her take.

"Bhen Ji, but 60 rupees is the nominal charge everywhere. I'm not even asking you that. Just 40! And look, I have also invested in a silver button for design, especially for you. Just 40." Usha's eyebrows tweaked when she spoke. Her disappointment of being underpaid choked her throat, and her mind was already making a list of all the household essentials they required.

"Arey, no, no, the work is not that good. Take 20 or nothing," the customer raised her voice.

Usha was afraid that she might lose other customers considering where the argument was geared toward. She knew her skills but praising her would mean giving her extra bucks. Criticizing gets the work done for cheap or free, for say. People, too, were aware of their needs and took advantage of that. But it was disheartening not to get acknowledged for her hard work.

"Okay, bhen ji, as you deem fit," she lost her spirits but walking home with something rather than nothing and watching her kids' faces kept her going.

It took some time, but the business took off, and she made at least 80 rupees daily, which she felt was enough for their needs. However, soon, their expenses increased manifold, and it was not just the kids' education and household items but also Ramesh's medical expenses. Though she knew all this, she didn't want to burden her loving husband. So, she worked harder and tried to manage with limited funds.

On days when the walls seemed to close in and the house was so small, she thought about the ones that made the four walls a home.

Fate could not have been crueler. The following day, they received a call from Ramesh's brother informing them about Roop Lal's sudden unexpected demise due to an unknown cause. This news caught Ramesh off guard, and he instantly fell to his feet and was aghast. He was an older man but energetic and fit. He would walk 30 km every day. Stuck in disbelief, Usha found it hard to digest the truth. Such a piece of news made Ramesh question life itself. A faceless void presented itself in his soul, and an inky gloom shrouded his countenance. Only so long could the mind persuade the heart to let go. Ramesh didn't want to invite any more trouble, and with a lot of pain, he accepted the death of his beloved father. He could now feel what Usha would've felt when she lost her father. This feeling was beyond someone else's understanding and could only be experienced if it happened to them. No amount of literature or words can ever make you feel the depth of what it feels like to lose a parent. Words are mere strings of letters, and beacons of sympathy can never ease the aching heart, and empathy can't encompass the magnitude of emotions that flood the bosom and leave one's soul barren. But the time at length arrived when grief was instead an indulgence than a necessity, and he had to jump this hurdle and move on. On one such day, deep in his thoughts and emotions, he started to think about what Usha would've gone through as everything went downhill, first with her father passing away, him falling sick, and moving away from their dream home. It left him with great respect and love for Usha, who never complained and loved him with all her being equally on their good days and bad.

Kiran was catching up with maturity much earlier than her age. She was fond of studying and loved reading books. She would spend hours cooped up in the corner of the house with a book in her hand. It became her solace and her sole companion. She felt words far beyond her understanding through merely printed letters inscribed on a pale-yellow paper page. She loved to study and learn new things, and she used to study every day with great enthusiasm. Subconsciously, she was living Usha's dreams of studying and becoming a successful person. It often brought tears to Usha's eyes to look at her daughter, who was filled with ambition and thirst to acquire knowledge. She saw a reflection of herself and could feel the little girl squealing with joy and opening her wings to take flight. So, Usha would save up extra money to ensure that Kiran had all the books she needed and never had to suffer.

On the contrary, Kanchan loved art just like her mother. She used to spend a lot of time making the best out of waste or painting mud vessels and beautifying everything. She liked to play and spend time with her friends and spent hours talking to them. Little Kunal was fond of machines, he tested his hands on anything and everything, and after dismantling an item, he would wonder how it worked. None of the household electrical items was spared from Kunal's tyranny, and to everyone's amusement, he rarely could bring back an item to its original working condition.

Kiran was relatively mature now that she had reached 8th grade, and Mr. Sharma, the former property dealer, had asked Kiran, who had laurels for her skill and knowledge, to tutor his children. Though apprehensive at first, Kiran saw it as a means to help her family and started training little children, and whatever sum she earned, she gave it to her mother. Kanchan, when she saw that Kiran had become independent, emulating her sister, she started tutoring too, and both girls helped the family uplift.

On one such day, after teaching students till 7 pm, both Kiran and Kanchan got ready at lightning speed as the family had to go to a relative's wedding. Usha wore a green saree which made her glow in her simplicity, and they reached the venue humbly clad. However, the moment they entered, all eyes were turned towards them, and expressions of contempt slowly made their way into their bulky makeup-laden faces.

"Where did you buy this diamond necklace from?" a curious voice pitched high and overtook the loud wedding music.

"Your saree looks gorgeous." Another voice made its way through the crowd.

"I've invested in stocks. Don't you think with its turnover, I would be able to buy another Rolex?" A well-pleased man rubbed against his palm in doubt.

"You know, I've been waiting for this wedding impatiently to finally get a chance to drape this beautiful saree." A boastful lady was giggling as if she had made the best comic. Preoccupied with their expensive attire, they could not garner the real reason behind their arrival, which was to pay respect to the bride and groom and to express their love for their family. The Bhatia's were greeted with fake smiles and disdain throughout the evening with a dose of dismissive taunts from the other family members, who were clad in expensive pieces to show off. At the same time, they had just reached the venue to pay their respect and show their love for their family. That day, Usha vowed that her children would be their family's charm.

Chapter

6
Darlings' 'D' Days

Chapter 6
Darlings' 'D' Days

The wheel of time rolled by rapidly, and her kids weren't kids anymore. Fifteen years passed, and her trio started earning a living for themselves and were keen on excelling in their careers. Usha would often sit on her usual wooden rocking chair and reflect upon the time when her trio engrossed her and sorted her help in settling every silly squabble, they had amongst themselves. She would smile to herself, recalling their salad days, and be nothing but happy for how they've built themselves now and become independent. They were working hard, which is the least to say, and Usha was doing her little bit, not out of necessity but from a space of familiarity.

It was hard to even think about Kiran and Kanchan getting married because they were a piece of her heart, albeit her whole heart, but she knew that it was vital for them to have their own families. She would often poke Kiran when she returned from her office, saying, "It's time for you to get married now. Tell us if you have someone in mind," and this statement would create in Kiran a hurricane; even the mention of marriage was enough to tick her off. Getting married, according to Kiran, actually means becoming a complete belonging to the other family. Getting married never crossed her mind and the notion of her life and space being shared with someone sent her jitters. She was so unready for everything a marriage could bring into her life. She wanted to wait for her siblings to follow her footprints to contribute to the household and uplift the family's financial status as she did.

Meanwhile, Kanchan would shy away and smile at such a statement, and a pink blush would slowly creep up her cheeks. Whenever Usha used to pay a visit to the gold shop, she would return and show all their jewels to her daughters, taking their silent approval and keeping them in mind. Little did they know it was her way of saving their earnings into a stable asset that could later be used for their marriage, as was the custom of that time. She kept a small sum each month to ensure a comfortable wedding for her children. She was happily doing all this while she had told her circle to be on the lookout for a match for her daughter, Kiran.

One day while Usha was handling her daycare Centre, a bell rang. She rushed towards the main door and opened it with a sudden metallic twang making their Godrej gate go wide open. There stood 5 feet tall, traditional Punjabi woman, Mrs. Kukreja, in front of her from their neighborhood. After assessing her head to toe, Usha joined her hands and asked her to come in. They sat on their new blue sofa which gave a whiff of regality into their humble living room, which was surrounded by building blocks and a random kitchen set lying here and there. Mrs. Kukreja didn't mind the hustle and bustle as she was a beneficiary of Usha's daycare service and often took care of her granddaughter. Usha ran to fetch her a glass of juice and came and sat down with her. She greeted Usha in her usual jolly manner. She started enquiring about her family and asked, "How are your daughters?" to which Usha replied, "They're doing well," and suddenly she sprang, "I've heard that Kanchan is working in a very reputed firm? She must be doing well. You have such successful children." Usha nodded and thought about the reason for her sudden arrival while being triumphantly proud of her daughters. Finally, Mrs. Kukreja stopped beating around the bush and came to the point, "Sister, I've got a match for Kanchan, "which caught Usha off-guard. She quickly processed this information and replied with genuine concern, "Sister, I think you're mistaken; I'm looking for a match for Kiran." Mrs. Kukreja shed a familiar look expressing her awareness of it too... Carefully mincing her words, she tried yet again to coerce Usha into accepting the offer for Kanchan, but Usha quite obstinately refused.

On the other hand, Usha had another storm to conquer, Kiran. She was steadfast that she wouldn't marry. Usha did receive some proposals, but neither Usha nor Kiran settled on even one.

On a Wednesday, when Kiran had returned from her tedious day at work, her mother had decided to dine out. The consensus was for Sagar Ratna, a popular south-Indian restaurant chain in North India, as the Bhatia household had an affinity for South Indian food. After hastily getting ready, they got into their Tata Indica, the second car they bought after saving for four whole years.

It was a humble silver-colored car, and Kunal loved his car dearly, to the point that he would make everyone clean their shoes before getting in and strictly prohibited any eating inside the vehicle. The weather was amazing that day, with fast-flowing winds, and it turned out to be a perfect day for an outing. So, with all windows down, they had set out for a cool, windy ride to a restaurant, which was an exciting experience not only for them but also for almost all middle-class households that resided in the heart of Delhi.

Usha started to sing her favorite song, *'Lag ja gale.'*[69] To match the lively atmosphere, it was a symphony to marvel at as it doubled their excitement and uplifted their moods. They arrived at the destination with joyous faces, as if they were rewarded in return for their long ride. But Kiran smelt something fishy. They went ahead and asked for a table for five. Seated and after comfortably ordering their *dosas*[70] and *dahivadas*[71] They started to talk to each other. Kanchan and Usha were sharing looks, for their mental porridge would be a party pooper for Kiran, and they were rubbing their hands like cute little satans. Finally, Kanchan started, "Kiran Didi, do you know we received a match for you." With that, a sly smile crept onto her face.

Meanwhile, all the colors faded, and all her joy was snatched from Kiran. Her mood turned upside down, and everything seemed to appear less appealing. Usha joined in. "Do you know his name is Raj, just like your favorite *Shahrukh khan*[72]?. Kiran made a poker face but soon plastered it with a fake smile. She was doing this to revolt against this possible mutiny, but they perceived it as a symbol of approval. Usha described the boy to

---

69 a popular Bollywood song of the 60's.
70 crisp, savory pancake.
71 fritters dunked in yoghurt.
72 A famous Bollywood actor from Indian cinema.

her in hopes that she could convince her, "He's fairly handsome and works in an IT firm." Though Kiran was annoyed that her parent's only preoccupation was her marriage, she sighed with resignation and agreed to meet this guy only to seal up their mouths. She returned home with an angrily bloated face.

Arrangements were made, and food was prepared to woo the potential son-in-law. Finally, he arrived on a black pulsar bike and removed his helmet with a macho charisma. It was a scene straight out of *Dhoom*[73], but unfortunately, placing him even close to *Hrithik Roshan*[74] was an exaggeration. Meanwhile, the whole Bhatia household was cooped up to the window facing exactly where he parked his bike. Everyone was curious to catch a look at him.

Soon, his anxious steps had led him to the front door, and he rang the doorbell slowly. Usha waited a few seconds before she opened the main gate to not look so eager. Kiran peaked from the kitchen; the moment her eyes fell on his face, a distant memory of a photograph crossed her mind, and this vast difference in his appearance and his so-called picture had been a comic scene. All decency and restraint left Kiran's mind, and she started to laugh at this hysterical figure that was standing at the door. That scenario was exactly like the viral meme template showing expectation vs. reality. She quickly wiped it off her mind thinking a book cannot be judged by its cover and invited him in for tea.

As it was the way of the world at that time: the two prospective candidates were sent to a room to interact for coming together

---

73 a popular Bollywood movie
74 a popular Bollywood actor from Indian Cinema

for this arrangement so that they could sign a deed which was heavily adorned and surrounded by relatives, heavy jewelry, and a crescendo of functions. So, they awkwardly sat on the bed and took turns looking at each other, hoping to think about a topic. All the while, Kiran was sealing her lips forcefully to prevent herself from giggling.

Raj broke the silence, "What do you do?"

and Kiran replied, "I work as an HR professional in a reputed firm."

"Do you love your job?" This question surprised him as he was expecting a superficial verbal repartee and not a battle of wits.

But he felt heavily challenged by this question and replied anxiously

"Well, I don't think I love it, but it's fine."

To call a spade a spade, Kiran was trying to evaluate Raj, for she thought it was important to love one's job to endure the constant toil and hard work for years.

"What are your hobbies? Do you love adventure?" Kiran threw a friendly question to make him not feel like an interviewee.

He gave a flat answer yet again after several unsuccessful attempts.

Kiran had understood that this man wasn't intellectually stimulating, and she needed to be challenged to thrive in a relationship.

Around this time, everything was working out in their favors: their health was good, and their families were flourishing.

Moreover, Ramesh was proud that his children were taking up the household responsibilities.

Some days later, Mrs. Kukreja reached out again, knowing little that she was about to be promoted from a neighbour to a relative because this time, Usha acceded to her proposal and asked for time to think. Meanwhile, her head was clouded with various thoughts as she was conflicted, and her mind was a two-way street. So, she decided to talk to Ramesh, who was worried about what others would think if the younger daughter got married before the elder one, but Usha had made up her mind by this time. She knew that others' opinions didn't matter. The only thing that mattered was a good match and her daughter's happiness. Ramesh and Usha, despite receiving limited education, had great wisdom, unlike the conventional society. The best match was more important than who got married first. Also, after observing Kiran's reluctance, she was sure that Kiran wouldn't marry anytime soon. So, it was decided, and they broke the news at teatime in front of the whole family. As soon as the news sunk in, Kanchan's face started glowing blush, and she shied away from the crowd. After Kanchan's approval, a meeting was planned with the guy.

The meeting was held in the Krishna temple in Janakpuri, where the Bhatia's and Nanda's interacted for the first time. The temple was huge, and as discussed earlier over the telephone, they decided to meet at 4 pm. Almost on time, the Bhatia's were excited to meet this guy who was so interested in Kanchan that he had sent the proposal twice. Kanchan was daydreaming about him, trying to decipher what he would look like, while Usha and Ramesh were engrossed in a casual conversation. Suddenly, a tall, well-built man clad in a solid light green shirt touched Usha's feet for blessings. She was surprised but instantly recollecting herself, gave him her blessings. When he looked up, he was sure to woo each one of the Bhatia family members with his charming and handsome face that had a hint of innocence preserved in the corner of his eyes. He had won Usha's heart with his kind manners, and this was the infamous Rahul Nanda. Her intuition suddenly hit her, suggesting that that guy would be perfect for her younger one.

Both the families conversed with gentle civility while Kanchan and Rahul were asked to take a walk to learn more about each other. Her pink dupatta was slipping down while sitting, and without paying enough attention to it, Kanchan quickly lifted it on her shoulder, and a low shy voice hit Rahul's ears.

"What do you do?"

Being equally self-effacing, he said, "I am an IT Professional."

When this little conversation race caught Usha's attention, she gave a gratified smile knowing everything would go well.

In the other group, pleasantries were exchanged. The family background was explored, and it looked like both families were comfortable with each other.

Rahul and Kanchan returned and joined the group. Their decision was evident on their faces making true the adage, 'The face is the index of the mind.' Looking at Kanchan's nervous smile, Usha felt that Kanchan had liked the boy, and as she turned her eyes towards Rahul, the same wobbliness had found its home on his innocent face too.

The family decided to think and exchange feedback in a day.

The next day, Usha received a call stating they liked their daughter and would be happy to have her as their daughter-in-law. Usha, who had already made up her mind, also replied affirmatively, and the good news was ready to be said to everyone. The agreement ceremony was planned for Sunday.

They had decided to tell the relatives to mark their calendars for their *Roka ceremony*[75] (It is an official announcement of your relationship in front of the world. It signifies that the bride and groom have accepted each other. Along with this, this is the first function when families officially meet each other.) On 7th December, a large gathering was planned for the roka as it was one of the first rituals for marriage for the Punjabis. Usha suddenly had many responsibilities to fulfil since Roka was traditionally done at the bride's place. Usha was flooded with a lot of arrangements to be taken care of. The day materialized in no time, and the house was decorated beautifully. There were yellow marigold flowers everywhere, from the entrance to the walls and the doors of each room. She had also organized the preparation of a three-course meal for all her guests. She had taken great pains to make the event perfect as it was a crucial one in Indian marriages.

The glow strengthened with the voices of the loud clatter of Kanchan's friends exclaiming, "Congrats, bub." Kanchan's eyes rolled out with excitement to reach out to the voice of Anuradha and Rohit, her dearest college mates. The to-be bride and the groom enjoyed the day and spent some time together. They interacted with each other's extended families. Kanchan's

---

75 Pre-wedding ceremonies in India.

cousins Sonu, Dheeraj and Rama were not excluded, for they set the absolute scenario on fire with their twinkling chuckles born out of teasing the couple. Kanchan and Rahul couldn't help but blossom throughout the ceremony. Usha, with her savings, had managed to organize a successful event and was highly satisfied as her daughter was getting married. Even though she had goosebumps that her favorite daughter would leave their home soon, she was still happy to see her settled.

Rahul often came to meet Kanchan, and whenever he entered their house, Usha used to greet him with her traditional delicacy *Aloo ka paranthas*[76]. His attachment with Usha proliferated as he often came to their house only to eat her aloo paratha.

It was a beautiful morning. The sky was clear, and a light breeze had kept their spirits up. Small birds wittering here and there composed a symphony that rang in everyone's ears. On the other hand, with high-spirited music, in a grand banquet hall, dressed in an exquisite red lehenga, Kanchan was making her way toward Rahul. She was the ultimate epitome of beauty and grace. All eyes were fixed on her, and tears glistened in the corners of Usha's eyes. The reality had finally struck her heart, and her emotions were in full flow. The traditional cliche *'din shagna da*[77]*'* played in the background, and the journey from the entrance to the stage was slow torture for Rahul, who couldn't wait to be her husband. Well, Kanchan was not the only showstopper at her wedding; Kiran, who wore a designer

---

76 a classical north Indian stuffed bread recipe made with wheat flour and spiced potato mash for stuffing.

77 A popular Punjabi track, sung during marriages. It means the auspicious day has arrived.

blue saree, was, of course, giving her competition, while Rahul looked dapper in a golden sherwani. Usha was so happy to look at her children; her eyes searched for Kunal, who was relatively young, for his mind prioritized being busy with his new friends and being careful with his attention being fixated on *Nandni*.

She was a beautiful tall woman with grey eyes, and her fashion sense was immaculate; her black suit had managed to turn more than a few heads towards her throughout the party, which made Kunal jealous. She could gauge anyone's attention because her aura was so radiant that no one could stop talking to her. Kiran, on the other hand, through the corner of her eyes, was watching all this, being a protective sister. She was curious to find out what was happening between the two. She tried to sneak in and listen to their conversation, but her attempts were up to no avail, so she calmed herself and waited with great anticipation for the day when Kunal would tell her about Nandni himself. Kiran, throughout the wedding, was busy talking to the guests and interacting with everyone, but by the end of the marriage, everyone was tired.

Usha's heart was whole at the same time; while Kanchan was leaving in a palanquin, she was experiencing a tussle of emotions. She tried to call out for Kanchan, but her throat choked, and Ramesh instantly shifted his gaze towards her. Noticing her ongoing struggle, he placed a hand on her shoulder, but he struggled and broke into tears. Usha looked at him, and a smile slowly took form on her lips. Both of them were giddy and to look at Kanchan leaving was too painful for them to articulate words. They saw their family of five turns six, yet some of them would now live away from them.

Slowly as things settled down, the fact that Kanchan was married started to sink in since the house wasn't the same without Kanchan's beautiful laughter and, of course, her patent omelette. On one such day, while Usha was having her usual cup of tea at the dining table, she felt unusually accomplished as the wedding was a sight to behold, but she was almost overthinking Kiran. All the things she had heard throughout the events were enough to make her worry about Kiran. So, she decided to reach out to a local matchmaker that evening. At the same time, their savings were almost exhausted, and Usha had to work harder to fill them back so that her other two children could be settled.

On Usha's birthday, the 15th of July, the family decided to have a little surprise party for Usha. Still, Usha was all the more surprised when the news that she was suddenly elevated to the position of a grandmother, staring at the 50 on her cake. She could visualize all those years going by so quickly, all in a matter of a second. She felt two generations senior, and of course, women and age are two things that don't go too well together, so in jest, she reached out towards the cake and shifted the candles to 05 because that's exactly how she felt then and for all the more years to come. She was so excited for the newborn baby that after congratulating the couple, the first thing her mind jumped to was knitting sweaters. It had been such a long time since she had made something for her children, and now that she was twice the mother, and her handiwork was supposed to be exclusive. She even started to collect the bedding, cot, and all the other things the baby would require.

Nearing two weeks overdue, Kanchan and Rahul went for a checkup, anticipating the doctor would finally hold a result showing a softened cervix. The baby was located where it wanted to be with cute little dilations. Kanchan felt emotional throughout the process and wished to be in her own mother's lap to ooze out her stored-up motherly emotions. Kanchan visited Usha after the hospital visit. The gazes of the mother-daughter duo spoke a lot and loudly rather than their words. Usha tried her best to provide financially with Kanchan's delivery, but it was not needed as it was handled double the amount from the Nanda's.

The Nanda's welcomed their grandson on 7th April. Kanchan being a devout worshiper of Lord Krishna named *Krishiv,* and Rahul being a synonym for Lord Shiva just added to its advantage; moreover, it meant that the child had qualities of both Krishna and Shiv. The household had frequent visitors filled with aunties and uncles showering the baby with various comments and blessings. The thought was of high spirit thanking God that the first child Usha's daughter Kanchan gave birth to is a male child. This inserted an anonymous sense of pride and achievement for Usha and Ramesh, for they exchanged gazes that only they could understand. The aura got diverted with the startling entry of Mrs. Kukreja, mami (Aunt) of Rahul hailing with bliss, "Haraay Usha! Krishiv is the spitting image of you!" Usha, on hearing this, felt elated, for she felt the true happiness of Mrs. Kukreja being bonded with their family.

After Krishiv's birth, Kanchan became a frequent visitor to the Bhatia household. She would often return to Usha, who would happily give her a welcome respite from her baby duties. Since he was the first child in the house, rightfully so, he was pampered and loved by all, but Kiran indulged him the most. She became his Santa and used to spend hours playing with him and his little toys.

Meanwhile, Kunal was doing well at his job and was almost always occupied by work or his beloved Nandni. Kunal ardently wanted to marry Nandni with the blessings of their family, and it would be safe to say that he had to work very hard to convince his family. He worked out a scheme to convince them one by one. It started by convincing Kanchan, and once she replied affirmatively, they colluded to convince the other three. As soon as Kunal heard the sound of a 'yes' taking form on his mother's lips, he ran with his phone and instantly called Nandni to set up a meeting between the families. The whole family was very excited, and when they met, everything worked out perfectly, and they decided to get married in February.

One day Kunal and Nandni went out for a dinner date at a fine restaurant. Kunal was beaming with happiness that he was finally getting married to the love of her life. But Nandni looked oddly quiet that day.

"Sir, your table for two is ready. Please come, Sir and Ma'am," the polite manager greeted Kunal and Nandni individually and showed them the way to a serene setting with a cozy ambience.

"Hey, all, okay?" Kunal whispered from behind while pulling a chair for her and waiting for her to sit.

"Umm, yes! Why do you ask?" Nandni pursed her lips while sitting on her chair.

"You look quiet today; what happened?" Kunal said as he got himself seated too.

"Kunal, I wanted to talk to you about this; I don't know where to start." Nandni pursed her lips.

Kunal felt sick from his stomach on hearing this. Is she calling off the wedding? What is going on? He thought.

"You're stressed too, the thing that you do from your lips," Kunal could make any moment lighter and make her laugh.

"You know, you can tell me anything. And start any way you want," he said as he took a sip of his water, hiding his nervousness.

"Kunal, the thing is, my father has borne some financial losses in business. And I don't want to burden him."

Ah! Shit, she is calling off the wedding, not a good reason, though! Man! Kunal's thoughts went haywire, and his palms went sweaty.

"So?" Kunal cleared his throat, hiding his anxiety; he took another sip of water.

"Could we arrange a simpler setting? And maybe prepone all of it?"

Prepone? Kunal felt amazing at that moment.

"What...? You scared me! Of course, yes, yes, a big yes to all of your ... 'conditions'! Kunal jumped from his chair and hugged her immediately.

"I can't wait to start my life with you," Kunal kissed Nandni on her forehead.

"Me too, Kunal. I'm so lucky to have you. I cannot believe

you will be so easy to talk to. You're so understanding." Nandni was overjoyed. Like every modern-day woman who thinks she is not a liability to her father, she felt relieved.

"Shut up, silly, prepone and a simple wedding? Are you kidding? Any day! Pleasure's mine really, can't wait! I love you!" Kunal chuckled as he hugged her tightly again and kissed her cheeks.

While everyone was busy celebrating the Christmas of 2008, Fate and the love bug had other plans. Kunal and Nandni were so in love that they could not wait another two months and decided to get married ahead of the planned date. They announced it to their families while the New Year feast was on in full flow. This caught Usha off-guard as she had prepared everything for the day, but this sudden change had thrown her off the field. The family fiercely resisted as they had already paid the booking amount for the venue and had to cancel on such short notice and prepone everything within three days of the announcement, which was already a difficult task.

Love's not only blind but is like a pair of noise-cancelling headphones, which numbs all your senses and just makes you 'humm' to its tune and dance on its melodic trance. So, when someone catches you lost in your muse, their tuneless eyes find you wandering and label you crazy; they haven't yet heard the tune that makes them dance without a view. The days passed as Kunal got stuck between petting his sister's baby and his mind overflowing with Nandni's honeyed words and thoughts. Kiran and Kunal sometimes had childish disputes on who will hold the baby first as soon as Kanchan reached home with Krishiv. On the other hand, Usha loved the sight and felt the calm waves of the dawned sea in her heart. Though mesmerized by looking at little Krishiv growing fast, she did not fail to work on the savings and preparations for her favorite son's wedding. Everyone had to finally agree to Kunal and Nandni's wishes, and the marriage was fixed for the 14th of January as it was an auspicious day. Clad in a royal blue sherwani, Kunal looked dashing and exuded confidence that came from his love for Nandni. As a tradition, when he rode the horse, Ramesh, with teary eyes and a heart full of pride, saw his younger one, who was still a child to him two days ago, suddenly becoming mature enough to get married. In a yellow tent filled with all the loving relatives and delicious food, the wedding was a beautiful affair since love was in the air and cupid had wooed every guest in one way or another. Its simplicity made it all the more special; the bride wore a maroon lehenga which matched perfectly with the blue sherwani. With her head held high, Nandni made her way towards Kunal, and a tear slipped out his eyes. His imagination was in no comparison to what he saw that day: a bride's charm was heightened by how they looked at each other and made everyone so excited and happy because love was meant to be cherished. Blushingly they both held each other's hand and felt exactly like the first day they had laid eyes on each other.

When the wedding rituals were complete, Kiran drove the newlywed to their *Kiran Garden* home. They couldn't keep their eyes off each other the whole ride as if a silent conversation was taking place between them, which Kiran was oblivious to.

The family was back to 5 yet again. Nandni made up for Kanchan's presence and being an introvert; she tried her best to mix up and become friends with Kiran and to be the best daughter for Usha. Meanwhile, Usha was worried as everyone in the family was talking about Kiran and blamed Usha for not getting the elder one married. The allegations stood to the extent that she did not want to let Kiran go as it would mean that the earning member of the house was moving out. Deep in her heart, she was aware of how difficult it was becoming with each passing day to get Kiran married, which made her anxious.

On the other hand, Kiran was stuck as a spinster, and marriage was nowhere among her dreams. With no other option in her foresight, Usha decided to consult some priests. Some of them told her to marry Kiran to an earthen pot, and some suggested a tree, while others shared rituals like leaving an open lock and key by Kiran's hand at a crossroad before the sun rose. Usha diligently fulfilled all of these rituals, hoping that by hook or crook, she'll get Kiran married, but luck wasn't in her favor; on the contrary, Kiran was getting diverted towards spirituality, which made Usha all the more anxious.

Nandni took the initiative with Kanchan to find a suitable match for her elder sister-in-law as she could no longer see her mother-in-law in pain every day, as society chided her with their inappropriate comments with no empathy. Kanchan took the liberty to create a Shaadi.com matrimonial account under Kiran's name and often sat and leisurely screened profiles and set review meetings with Kiran, which Kiran would instantly reject. So, Usha told them to set up the meetings straight away and not give Kiran the chance to say no.

Kiran was an HR Manager in a startup company in Noida. Her routine was packed: she used to get up at six and leave home by 7 with Ramesh, who would drop her at the metro station, and return at around 9 pm with her father, who would be waiting for her at the metro station every day. Though silent, Ramesh spoke out his thoughts louder, his calm breath and patient eyes conveying that he feels more comfortable and prouder that Kiran takes the lead and poses as a parental figure for her siblings. He wants nothing more than that.

On a sunny afternoon, while having lunch with her colleagues in the cafeteria and indulging in some chitter-chatter, Kiran received a call from Kanchan, who informed her that she had spoken to a potential match and had fixed up a call with him and requested her to talk to him politely. Kiran was left shocked, but she had no other option. Within an hour, she received a call from this said match. The relatively heavy and mature voice asked her, "Is this Kiran...?" Kiran confidently chimed, "Yes, I am."

"Well, your sister gave me your number," the male voice responded.

"Yes... she told me," ... Kiran said...

"My name is Vineet Tandon, and I work as a Manager of HR with a fortune five organization."

Kiran misinterpreted his introduction as showing off and responded. "I work as a Manager HR in a reputed automobile company," asserting her designation.

Kiran, as usual, tried to get rid of him as she did with all other potential suitors. But she was pleasantly surprised at the call, and the person behind the alluring voice started to grow on her slowly. There was something about him that made her feel comfortable and calm. It was as if he was there to rewrite the stars of Kiran. The conversation continued, but Kiran had still not warmed up to the idea of marriage and continued to battle, hoping to scare him away.

She said, "I don't eat non-veg, " anticipating his aversion.

Vineet replied, "That's fine."

Kiran continued the usual, "I am XX. What's your age?"

Vineet replied, "I am XX."

Kiran thought she had found the master stroke, "We have an age difference."

But alas, Vineet replied, "Age is just a number."

Kiran found him flattering and open-minded, so she decided to continue the conversation. She said her customary goodbyes and saved his number on her phone.

That day while returning home in the metro, she received a call from Vineet.

"Where are you?" asked Vineet

(Thinking how dumb he was as she had already informed him that she travels by metro) she replied, "In a metro."

"Of course, I know... I mean, where have you reached?" was his reply, and Kiran, mentally laughing, replied, "It has stopped at Rajeev Chowk, CP." *(metro station spot in the heart of the city, Delhi)*

He instantly asked her to get down, and Kiran, without thinking twice (with a blank mind), got down from the metro.

Vineet was on his way to meet Kiran at the metro station.

It was the last day of the Olympics in India, and the closing ceremony was being held around that time; many screens were put up for display as it was a matter of pride for India. Walking out of the metro station and clearly perplexed and wondering if the call was just a joke, Kiran decided to walk towards a screen to watch the ceremony, if nothing else. Suddenly, she heard her name being called out and instinctively turned. The same voice that soothed her a while back emanated from a Maruti Swift. Kiran joined Vineet in the car, and the moment she became comfortable, he spoke in a Bollywood-like fashion, "So finally we meet!" and chirped. Lifting her head to give a smile, Kiran noticed his deep brown eyes that glowed like a pool of honey with a sense of depth that comes from maturity. A fit figurine adorned in a light blue polo shirt and fairly tall enough, it seemed to have greeted Kiran, and she instantly forgot to smile and was pleasantly distracted. Regaining her composure, she gave a slight nod of approval and maybe a little smile.

He looked at her with questioning eyes and asked, "Where do you want to go from here?"

Kiran's fight or flight response had kicked in, and the adrenaline was going through her body. Assessing the situation, she started to find ways to run off, but nothing seemed worthy, so sighing in resignation, she decided to raise the white flag against flight and chose to fight. While waiting for her, Vineet thought now that she was in his car, she had to at least have a coffee with him. So, he drove towards Costa Coffee while the radio filled up the awkward silences, and with a few romantic songs here and there, he had managed to ease Kiran's anxiety a bit, and they had enough basic information to cover in this short 'interview.'

After ordering an americano and a cappuccino, Kiran noticed Vineet taking out a pen and writing something on tissue paper. He said, "I earn XXXX Rs, and how do u plan to run a house if we plan to get married (in his mind, he was giving a challenge to a candidate to get rid of her). Kiran took it as a challenge and answered with no plans of being defeated, "I earn YYYY RS a month, and a total of two makes ZZZZ Rs per month, and if we do a breakdown of expenses. We can save 10%, and this can be used to book our first house."

Vineet was impressed and had complete faith in her presence of mind, while Kiran took it sportingly as she was finally enjoying this game now that she was being intellectually stimulated. The evening came to a close soon, and he dropped her off at her metro station.

The moment Kiran entered the threshold, Nandni was waiting for her and asked, "How was the boy?" and Kiran, with a surprised look, replied, "How do you know?" Usha interrupted this conversation, unable to hold back her horses, and asked her directly. Kiran said, "I neither like nor dislike him." Usha smiled since this was the first time, she hadn't outrightly said no.

Nandni insisted Kiran show her a photograph of the boy, and Kiran switched on her laptop to search for Vineet on Facebook and showed it to Usha and Nandni. Upon a good 5-second look at the photograph, Nandni responded, "His eyes looked like Guruji." and Usha nodded in agreement." Kiran was still a little confused but went to her room and gazed at the picture of guruji, the well-known spiritual leader she followed and whose portrait was in her room across the bed. She retook one good look at Vineet's picture and instantly felt connected, slowly surrendering her heart and believing in the conviction that he was the 'one.' She was the one who could for sure take care of her parents and was fairly broad-minded and intellectual. She loved the way her intelligence was debated by the others.

A little later, after having dinner, she told Usha that she agreed with Nandni and would marry him as long as he agreed to the relationship. Kanchan called around that time, and she was also given the good news and informed that she had cunningly conspired about the meeting.

Kanchan informed her mother that the boy hails from Kanpur and lives with his relatives in Delhi. He is an HR professional. He has a working mother, and Vineet's father left early. Usha was happy that the boy had achieved such great heights in a few years and all that with his hard work. He was intelligent and responsible, beyond his age, and this security made Usha feel confident in giving away her daughter. Since Kiran and Vineet were not only in the same profession but were equally educated, all the other information she received from Kiran about their thought process, rich heritage, and educational background made Usha feel that he was perfect.

At the same time, Kunal had taken the responsibility of reconstructing the house according to Usha's vision, and the family temporarily shifted to a nearby place. Vineet's family was invited for a formal meeting between the families. Usha was anxious as the thoughts of the temporary house clouded her mind, and she was worried about what the boy's family would think about them knowing that they were staying in rented accommodation. Ramesh caught her between one of these overthinking sessions as the lines on her forehead revealed her worry. Upon learning about the cause, he consoled her, "Don't worry, Usha. They wouldn't think about such petty things. Some things are more important than just concretes and cements."

It was a rainy morning, and Usha was worried about the weather and wondered if they would still come today. A ring of the bell made her rush to check their arrival. Upon opening the door, their smiling faces had worked magic on Usha's restless heart. After being seated and talking a little with Ramesh and Usha, Usha called out to Kiran, and she served tea to Vineet's mother, uncle, aunt, sister, and cousins. Usha asked her to take a seat near Vineet's family. For the first time, she saw her confident daughter trembling with nervousness. Kiran came and sat near Vineet, but her heart pounded much more than it did the day of her first interview. Vineet's mother cleared her throat, and Kiran looked up in anticipation, wondering what she would ask, but all her worries vanished when his mother made Kiran feel comfortable and just wanted to know her better. The fact that his mother was so amiable and sweet made Usha feel lucky, as well as proud. A few other questions about her favorite food and hobbies followed, and his family placed a box of sweets on her lap as a sign of acceptance of the marriage proposal. Usha asked Kunal to bring the necessary *sagan*[78] as a token of their acceptance, all went well, and the moment the boy's family stepped out of the house, Usha was jumped; it was as if, finally, her penance had given her a fruitful return.

---

78 an auspicious signal, usually an envelope with some money

She excitedly called all her siblings and family to provide them with the good news. The next day, relatives started to pour in one after another to congratulate the family. The entire family couldn't hold their double happiness within as Dheeraj got engaged, and his marriage was just a week before Kiran's engagement. The family was loaded with fiesta mode as Subash and Ramesh both had their precious one's wedlock, and their emotions were more relatable as in their kite flying high days.

Usha finally felt at peace that now all her responsibilities would be over with Kiran getting married and breathed a sigh of relief.

The two families decided to have two functions for the marriage wherein the engagement was to be held in Delhi to accommodate all the Bhatia relatives. Finally, the marriage was to be held in Kanpur.

Usha wanted to explain how she felt about her daughter, so as she wrote a few lines for her daughter's wedding card, she scribbled a few sentences. That was elaborated upon on the wedding card.

Betiyaan (DAUGHTERS)

Daughters are like a drop of Dew,

Daughters are cherished by their uncle and beloved by their father...

Daughters understand their parents' distress.

Sons may only light up one household at a time.

The daughters are a of pride for both clans.

A true pearl is a daughter if a diamond is a son.

Daughters pass through the briars, but they also bloom, brightening the path of those around them.

Even though society thinks daughters are a part of someone else's family, they are actually much more of your own than sons.

The sons are the eyes, and the daughters are the lids.

Having Daughters Is Really just the Summation of Life

From ages, we have been told that a daughter is someone else's asset,

but have realized today how painful it is to say goodbye to your loving daughter

What a peculiar connection there is between misery and joy.

My shadow is bidding me farewell...

All of you, please join the occasion to bless our darling daughter "Kiran,"

-Mom and Dad

Betiyaan

Os ki boond si hoti hai Betiyaan, Papa ki pyari aur Tau-Chacha ki dulari hoti hai Biyaan,

Maa-Baap ke dard main humdard hoti hai Betiyaan, Roshan Karega beta to bas ek hi kul ko,

Do-do kulon ki laaj hoti hai Betiyaan, Heera agar hai beta to saccha moti hai Betiyaan,

Kaanto ki raah par chalti hai Betiyaan, Auro ki rah mein phool banti hai Betiyaan,

Kehne ko parai amanat hai Betiyaan, Par beton Se bhi badhkar apni hoti hai Betiyaan,

Beta hai aankh, to palak hai Betiyaan, Jeevan Ka Saransh hai Betiyaan,

Beti dhan paraya hota, yeh hum sunte aaye, Dard vidai ka kya, aaj samajh mein aaya,

Gam our khushi ka rishta kaisa yeh ajeeb hai bhai, Meri parchhai mujhse le rahi vidai.....

Aap sabhi ki ladli "Kiran" ko aashirwad dene zaroor padhariye.....

.... MOM & DAD

While the engagement preparations were in full swing around the same time, Dheeraj (Subhash and Kamlesh's son) was getting married a few days before Kiran's engagement too, which threw Usha in a frenzy as she had to manage two functions at the same time. While Ramesh and Subhash were elated as two of their favorites were tying their knots. Usha's stress knew no bounds, so she decided to delegate her responsibilities and gave Kiran and Vineet the accountability to buy stuff for themselves for their engagement ceremony and the wedding, which made them feel responsible on the one hand and ecstatic on the other so that they can spend more time together.

It was a sunny morning, and Old Delhi was bustling as always. Vineet and Kiran were together in hopes of fulfilling their duties and helping out their mother. Clad in a green and white, Kurta Kiran exuded the glow that comes along with the preparation of marriage. She looked divine, with her eyes fixed on the show window of a store. Vineet turned himself towards the window, too, following Kiran's line of sight and called out to her sister to stop as he believed that Kiran had found something. All the while, Kiran's eyes were fixated on a White pearl-based saree that had initially hypnotized her; she could imagine her mother-in-law looking divine in the exquisite piece. They entered the shop, and almost all the designs were fresh and new. She asked for the pearl white saree while Vineet's sister asked to look at some bridal pieces for Kiran.

The shopkeeper proposed a sequence-based, blue-colored traditional skirt and blouse and mentioned it would look beautiful and pretty different for the bride. Though it was his usual business tactic, it still sounded pretty honest, for the bride was glistening with a bold pink tinge on her soft cheeks with all her marriage dreams. Kiran initially loved the lehenga, but the thought of wearing red slowly found a place in her mind. She thought that her mother would want her to wear a red lehenga, so she found herself with a problem.

Since Vineet was pretty modern for that time, he agreed with the shopkeeper and wanted Kiran to wear some modern piece that could do justice to her bold streak. So, Kiran finally removed all her prejudices and decided to wear the blue lehenga. They also bought matching bangles, jewelry, and shoes for her.

On the other hand, Vineet was very particular about his ensemble, and they entered a shop that sold formals and shortlisted some formal three-piece suits that were perfect for him. But they could not choose even after much deliberation and decided to call Usha, who had a very modern dressing sense. So, taking Usha's opinion into account, they went with her choice of a dark grey suit with a pink shirt which was the majority consensus.

The day of the engagement arrived in no time. Usha was flustered with all the boxes in her hand and the other knick-knacks. Kunal and Nandni followed closely behind her. Nandni was, of no doubt, a double swift flying jet on the land, for she devoted herself to being a right hand for Usha. She helped herself to shop for the wedding with utmost care and calculations. Keenly prepared giveaway clothes for relatives, minute items of kitchen, beddings, clothes for Kiran, taking care of Ramesh's medicines, planning for wedding card distribution with Usha, cooking, etc. The trail came to an abrupt stop, Kunal noticed Usha looking at the large banner that displayed Kiran and Vineet's portrait, a hasty picture they had taken time out from their busy schedules, but it turned out to be perfect. After admiring the decoration that speaks louder than the friends and relatives buzzing like busy bees. The trail went inside. The venue was large and gilded with orchids at each corner. All relatives and Friends of the Bhatia's were invited, and it was a magnificent arrangement done by Kunal.

After all, this was the last wedding of the house, and Usha and Kunal wanted it to be a grand affair and a benchmark for everyone they knew. The food counters ranged from Indian, Mexican, Chinese, and Lebanese cuisines, with liquor served freely to all the guests.

The valet parking was welcoming and arrived hassle-free for all the guests. They were greeted with a wide range of cocktails and snacks. There was a counter for "Paan," too, an Indian mouth fresher that everyone loved to devour after food.

All the relatives complimented Usha for the beautiful arrangement as they were one of a kind and had never seen before. Something nobody expected from Usha. Relatives were amazed by the fairy tale arrangement for Kiran's engagement ceremony.

All seniors of the Bhatia family were standing with their hands joined at the entrance as a gesture of warm welcome for the Tandon's. The ceremony began with "tilak" for Vineet. Then, Vermillion was blended with holy water, and Kunal inoculated a decorated dot on Vineet's forehead, followed by Usha, who repeated the same with all her love for her son-in-law. Further, Usha made him wear a gold chain, put many gifts on his lap, and handed over gifts for the family members to Vineet's mother.

Kanchan and Nandni walked with Kiran to bring her to the stage where Vineet was sitting and waiting for his bride-to-be to join in as soon as Kiran joined the scene. The ceremonies from the Tandon's began in full vigor and in a similar fashion to that of Vineet. Kiran was made to wear gold bangles and silver anklets.

Post the rituals, all the guests came onto the stage one after the other to bless the new-be couple and get their photographs clicked. Watching this from a distance, Usha thanked her stars for giving her this extraordinary experience of witnessing such a mammoth, unbelievable arrangement. She couldn't believe her eyes watching the brightest and boldest star of her life sparkling afar on the stage. This feeling of fulfilment made her forget all the struggles she had endured. Inside her heart, Usha felt blessed to have a son like Kunal, who made all this possible and for uplifting her spirits.

****

It was a Sunday morning, and the doorbell rang. As Usha rushed to open the door, she was pleasantly surprised to see Vineet standing with a bouquet of assorted flowers.

He touched her feet and exclaimed, "Happy Anniversary, Mumma."

Usha cheerfully welcomed him inside, questioning, "how did you know."

"You are my mother, and I am supposed to know everything

about you." Vineet's reply had won her heart, and she felt he was a perfect father figure for Kiran's younger siblings too.

They arranged a cake and celebrated their parents' anniversary with lots of love.

The morning was cheerful, and Usha and Ramesh clicked lots of pictures with their would-be son-in-law. Kanchan and Rahul visited with Krishiv, who had arrived to celebrate the anniversary of his grandparents and bought a little chocolate for them. Kunal asked Usha what she wanted as her anniversary gift, to which Usha responded, "let us get the house repair work completed quickly; I want to go back to the house before Kiran's marriage."

It was an arduous task to be achieved in a month. However, Kunal was determined to make it happen like cloud nine for his mother. The days passed in a blur as Usha was busy with the wedding arrangement and was nervous as the wedding was to be held in Kanpur. While drafting the wedding cards, Usha was asked to express her feelings for her daughter, and she wrote a few lines that were crafted onto the wedding card before they went for printing. The excerpt was a little yet profound surprise for Kiran, with deep insight and multiple meanings.

Kunal had spent all his hard-earned money on that one house, and each aspect of it became so precious to Usha and Ramesh, and they were so proud and lucky to have such a great son.

The sky was delightful that day, and the green of the trees was a little sharper, for it wanted to convey something intelligent and robust, blurring the past happenings. Spring had made its way into the flower-laden streets of Delhi. On such a March morning in 2011, Usha and her family shifted to their newly constructed home in Kiran Garden. The sunshine had gathered overhead, reflecting their happy mood on sighting their home, a small three-story building that Kunal had built with Usha's instructions. When they stepped foot into the compound, and after taking one look at the house, everyone instantly fell in love with it. The cool breeze, the vibrant walls, the fresh paint, and the earthy smell of the brick house immediately filled them with incomparable joy. Usha's life inspired the house, and the home was an inspiration for all the family members, just as Usha was.

The care and time taken in choosing, building, and furnishing every part of the house was an exciting period for Usha as she started to imagine all the beautiful moments, they would spend in this newly constructed home together with their big happy family.

As Kiran's wedding was around the corner and there was a load of work to settle in the new house, Usha's inherent capability to mould herself according to the situation and take up any challenge took the forefront. She multitasked, managing wedding arrangements and setting up her new house at the same time.

Soon floral decorations and string lights were being put up outside the house, which served as a cordial invitation and had set up the mood days before the guests started to show up. A day before the housewarming, Usha looked into making the necessary arrangements for her new house. As the function was planned at the beginning of March, the weather was pleasant and was perfect for making the guests comfortable. A percolation was kept to worship goddess Durga as a housewarming ceremony. It is a religious watch kept during regular sleeping hours, during which prayers or other ceremonies are performed. It is a particular type of ritual in which devotees congregate, sing devotional songs, and praise some of the other deities, especially Goddess Durga, keeping awake the whole night.

All guests blessed Usha and her family for the two crucial events (the housewarming and Kiran's upcoming wedding).

The wedding rituals began with the Henna application (which was sponsored by Tandon's for Kiran), and little girls from the relatives joined in for the event. Usually, in their family, henna was considered a bad omen. Hence it was sponsored by the Tandon's. Even Usha desired to get a beautiful design made on her hands, but she stuck to the customs, while Kiran's hands were beautifully decorated with henna that turned out to be the perfect red. On a small corner on her ring finger was Vineet's name drawn in cursive. Kiran kept looking at it and was planning to challenge him to find the name as it was so small that it could instantly trick the human eye.

As the wedding was planned in Kanpur, Usha and Ramesh's siblings and their families, along with the Nanda's and Sharma's families, travelled to Kanpur via train. All the travel arrangements were done by Kunal with Usha's guidance. Whereas Kunal himself planned to drive down as there was a lot of stuff he needed to carry, which would've been a hassle on the train.

Two days before the wedding, as everyone gathered at the railway station to board the train to Kanpur, Usha was quite nervous while handing over tickets to the travelers. She had a suspicion that something was wrong. To her utter surprise, the tickets were fewer. She checked with Kunal, and they realized that the number of travelers was more than the planned numbers. Looking at his nervous mother, Kunal took charge and asked some members to travel with him by road. There was only a shortage of one ticket now, and that's when Usha told Kunal that she would travel without a seat.

Kunal was apprehensive about the idea and insisted she joins him in the car. However, Usha didn't want to leave her relatives alone during the travel. She was hell-bent on travelling by train only with all her guests. She was the host, and she was not okay with the idea of leaving the guests alone during travel. Kunal checked the tickets counter and could not get access to the seat; however, all he could get was a permission ticket to travel without a seat.

It was a difficult night for Usha as her legs were aching badly. The 8-hour journey was a nightmare for her, but it didn't deter her spirit. After all, it was her daughter's wedding, for which she had been so excited for so long. As the train stopped at Kanpur Central station, Vineet and his cousins were at the railway platform to welcome Usha and her family. Usha was touched by his gesture and was elated by the fact that Vineet had joined her to provide a warm welcome to the Bhatia family. She found him to be a well-mannered boy as he always showed up for everyone. Vineet could make out that Usha was tired, took charge of the situation and managed the transportation for everyone to reach comfortably to the guest house with the help of his cousins. He took Usha with him in his car and was concerned for her, questioning her, "why did she bother herself so much for the travel."

As everyone reached the guest house, breakfast was already arranged for them courtesy of Vineet to provide respite to the guests from Delhi. During the breakfast, Usha requested everyone to have some rest and informed them the evening was hosted by Tandon's as a welcome for them.

On the same day, there was a cursory customary function followed by the wedding the next day. The Bhatia family was entirely impressed by all that Vineet had done for them and the beautiful arrangements he had made for his bride-to-be. The wedding was a lavish affair with delicacy, an inward expression of the groom's love for the bride and her family, and it was even better than the engagement ceremony. Kunal, Nandni, and Kanchan had prepared a dance performance, and halfway into it, they forgot the dance steps, so Kiran stepped in and took charge, which gave a delicate blow down through the wedding hall, and they enjoyed themselves to the fullest. While sitting and greeting the relatives, Vineet always ensured that Kiran was comfortable and that she had eaten, and his concern made Kiran blush. Kiran's lehenga became a style statement, and the whole family was in awe because it was bold at that time to wear a modern stone rich maroon heavy lehenga than a simple red, but everyone appreciated it because she carried it with immense grace and beauty. Even Vineet felt starstruck after looking at his beautiful bride and thanked the stars they had met. The affair was a success, and everyone happily returned to Delhi in two days.

Chapter 7
Proud Progeny

Chapter 7
Proud Progeny

Soon after Kiran's wedding, Usha became preoccupied with managing and decorating her newly constructed home, as well as hosting kitty parties with her friends in Kiran Garden.

While life went on as usual, managing the house, chatting with friends and relatives, and ensuring Ramesh's well-being, Usha was enjoying and feeling relieved that all of her children are settled in their lives.

Few months later, on a Wednesday morning, Usha receives a call, and Kiran's exuberant jumping and shouting can be heard on the other end of the phone...Usha's face was puzzled, not knowing to grasp the exact scenario at the other end. Usha tried and failed to question her daughter as there was no gap of breath like the cluster of autumn leaves during fall. Kiran was incapable of putting her thoughts into words, but after some time to calm down, she spoke...

Mom....

Catch your breath first... responded Usha with a concerned tone

Yea... yea...

All ok with you and at your home?

Yes... Mom... All good... have something to share...

Thank God... I was scared...hearing you breathless... responded Usha...

No... all good...

So, you got a pay raise?...

No.... o.... o... you are going to be a grannie...soon...

On the other side of the phone... Usha's lips were open wide with exclamation and pleasant surprise,

Kiran obliquely wanted her mother to expect a bit tiny mouth that was about to call her 'Nani'. Usha got completely drenched with no rain under the roof. She was out of words where she felt the whole world as a tiny insect under her feet.

This was more of music to Usha's ears, and she immediately regained consciousness and started chirping with joy and carrying sweets to the Tandon's house as soon as she heard it. No words could express how happy she was, but in the back of her mind, she was hoping Kunal would have a family of his own. While she was making the necessary preparations for Kiran, she kept this worry in the back of her mind.

Kiran would frequently visit them, and Nandni would take excellent care of her and be overjoyed. When Kiran was nearing the end of her pregnancy, Kanchan would come in to assist. She would spend a lot of time with her mother because she needed her support, but Vineet's mother would also take great care of her and make her a lot of *'pinnis'*[79] to eat. She always ensured she ate a nutritious meal and was never left alone. Vineet was her rock throughout the pregnancy, not only managing work

------

79 A dessert made from Indian ghee, wheat flour, jaggery, and almonds

but also ensuring that Kiran's wishes and whims were met without an if or a but.

Kiran was pregnant, and her baby measured big yet safe. Kiran can't help but think about how her life of marriage with Vineet was about to change with the arrival of this cute little one. She weaved a million dreams about how she and Vineet are predestined to raise the baby together. Kiran also grew anxious, as if it were a part of the pregnancy struggle. Though it was painful at times, she still loved it. She loved the baby kicks inside her stomach and the smoothening care from her mother, Vineet, and siblings. Her expectations grew as her days grew older.

Kiran went in for a checkup right before her due date, expecting the doctor to discover a dilated cervix and the beginnings of labor. Nothing!

The doctor recommended that she hold off for one more week. She was sick of being sent home from the hospital after each visit. While returning home, Kiran made the decision to remain as active as possible until baby decides to come out of her.

Five days later, on a quiet Saturday evening in June, which had become quite noisy due to Kiran's constant shrieks, the Tandon's welcomed a beautiful baby boy who was as red as a rose.

His cries filled the room and Vineet busted into tears of relief and joy. He turned his glossy eyes to Kiran and in a voice, that's almost broken he tells her they have a beautiful son. Through her exhaustion, she smiled and took her gaze away from his face to take in the baby that was placed on her bare skin.

She began to cry the sweetest tears she'd ever known at that moment, all the pain of the previous moments melting away. He was only a day old. His smile was as sweet as a summer strawberry, filling Vineet and Kiran's hearts with sunshine they didn't know existed.

He was named *Abeer,* which means 'gulaal,' as he colored everyone's lives with happiness and joy. The little Abeer had no idea what amount of pleasure he could bring with his tiny lips producing such a dazzling smile. The entire surrounding melted like massive, tall walls of ice.

Usha was by her side throughout their entire hospital stay; she ensured that her daughter was comfortable and that everything was taken care of properly. She constantly pestered Kiran with too many caring and devoted questions. "Have you sanitized Abeer's sipper bottle?" she would ask. Before Kiran gathered up her strength to utter an answer, Usha would continue,

"Have you disposed of yesterday's diapers?"

"Have you taken the medicines I kept beside you this morning?"

Questions would follow up with her sweet yet strict orders, "Go take an early bath, for Abeer's surroundings must be kept clean and tidy." Kiran's silence made her wonder if she was audible enough. Without taking a breath nearing Kiran's room, she would continue, "Kiran do you hear me?"

Kiran, with a kiddish yet kind smile, said, "yes... Yes... Mom... I hear you. Everything is perfect."

Abeer's babble interrupted the mom-daughter duo as if

he was affirming his Nani that his mom had completed her routine chores.

His, Whoa! Whoa! with angelic smile melted Usha but little did she have time to enjoy her fav grandson's acts.

Usha spent a lot of time at their house and assisted in the upbringing of Abeer, even though Vineet's mother was a working professional at LIC in Kanpur. She was present when Abeer uttered his first words and took his first steps. She assisted Kiran in running the household to free up time for her to go to work.

"Nani... Dadi... Nani... Dadi... "Abeer would call out with his little stumbling baby talk. Both Usha and Vineet's mother would turn to Abeer yearningly.

Both wanted to hold Abeer's first priority for them. "Abeer called for me!" Vineet's mom would say.

"No... Noo. It was 'Nani,'" Usha would say with proud stress. And both would laugh following Abeer's clatter.

Usha felt lost at the sight of Abeer growing up. Right from him turning around in bed, scrolling with his tiny legs and hands with his unique baby chortle to the point when Abeer started uttering vivid baby babble. Usha couldn't wait to see Abeer's mouth filled with the word "Nani."

Nani.... Nani... Usha's face would light up with happiness whenever she heard little Abeer repeating "Grandmom" repeatedly. Then, Abeer started to reveal his cute little steps that created an in-depth stamp in every heart around. He began to hold things with those tiny little fingers, for those non-living things did not want to be released from Abeer's grasp. Nani and Abeer liked to throw colorful balls at each other while playing in a pool of balls. Abeer appeared like a little colorful fish enjoying the pool with its alluring fins moving sideways and under. The evenings were filled with merriment and laughter at Kiran's home in Indirapuram, thanks to Abeer's rides on the swings. It used to feel to Usha and Ramesh as if they were reliving Kiran's childhood all over again.

Ramesh would call Abeer, "My little Kiran!" With his tired yet energetic voice. It was apparent to everyone's notice that his face lit up bright whenever he held Abeer.

Managing Abeer with Kiran and spending time in Kiran Garden House seemed to pass quickly. While this was going on, Usha kept busy with kitty parties, and her favorite topic of conversation with her friends was the time she spent playing with two of her grandchildren. It felt as if Usha had lost all her rates of stress and depression she had so far. Krishiv and Abeer became the best medicine that held the credibility of curing anything and everything.

When Kiran and Kanchan would visit with their respective sons, the Bhatia residence was always bustling with vibrant colors and energizing activity. Usha usually gets busy cooking their favorite dishes for her daughter and son-in-law and the little munchkins before her daughters arrive.

With Krishiv and Abeer's presence, the house would be filled with the excitement and noise of little children waiting to see their grandparents. Usha fed them once every 15 minutes, and Kiran and Kanchan could relax because the kids were staying at grandma's house, where they didn't have to worry as much about the meals the children ate.

Krishiv and Abeer covered Grannie, and they were in her own home at the time. At this point, her favorite way to pass the time was by taking out her black piggy bank in the shape of a water tank. The money in the piggy bank consisted of various old and new coins, including one paise, five paise, ten paise, 25 paise, 50 paise, 1 rupee, 2 rupees, and 5 rupees.

Krishiv would exclaim, "Nani... Nani...It's five paise."

"No, it's 25 paise..." Usha said.

"Nahi nani! It's five paise..." repeated Krishiv.

"Yes, my son, all for you... "Usha would exclaim with a smile.

She kept Krishiv occupied by challenging his mathematical abilities, and with Abeer, she would play a game in which they would take turns giving and receiving coins from each other's fists.

Kiran and Kanchan joke that their mother had regressed to childhood with their sons. Usha wished to stop ageing just to feel and pamper the kids with the unchanging firmness in her heart and soul.

Because Abeer is the younger of the two, Usha would constantly hold him in her lap. Usha would also take Abeer to the market and introduce her to her other friends. Walking with her grandson in her arms, she felt a sense of pride and joy in her life. Friends of Usha used to grab her attention, saying she had become a Nani and asking when she anticipated becoming a *dadi.*[80].

---

80 Grandmother (Son's kids).

This prompted Usha to express her desire to Kunal and Nandni to become a grandmother to their children. Usha's desire had put silent pressure on Kunal and Nandni to become parents. Though Nandni never affirmed directly, she blushed every time Usha mentioned the baby. Kunal was determined to do anything in his capacity to make his mother happy, and Nandni was on board with his line of thinking the entire time.

Time flew by, and Usha did not leave any stone unturned in her prayers to the almighty to grant her wish to become the grandma of Kunal's children. Abeer and Krishiv, on the other hand, continued to be her favorite playmates and the apple of her eye. It appeared as if Abeer and Krishiv had grown up a lot within the flip of a second. They seemed taller than before with sparkling eyes and milk-tinted cheeks.

Each Year was welcomed with prayers for the well being of kids and Ramesh. Usha's desire to be a grandmom for Kunal's children, on the other hand, grew steadily stronger over time.

On a pleasant morning where the clouds were trying so hard to lay their sponges over the beaming rays of the sun, Usha was once again given the fantastic news that Kiran was expecting a child shortly after Abeer turned three years old. Naturally, Usha was delighted to hear the word, and she secretly harboured the desire for Kiran's family to be finally completed with the addition of a daughter.

Months decided not to stop anywhere as if they were eager for the upcoming babies of the Bhatia's. Kiran herself couldn't believe that she was almost halfway there with her second baby. It sounded magic how fast the weeks had been flying by. Kiran's second pregnancy was completely different from her first pregnancy. She felt tired of handling this pregnancy with the presence of a toddler.

Despite Usha's anxiety and desire to become a dadi, Usha was overjoyed by the news of Kiran's pregnancy as it would allow her to experience the joys of her childhood all over again with a little bit of a difference from what she shared with Abeer. That which Usha had been hoping for the past three years had finally come to fruition when Nandni told her she was expecting, and she was overjoyed.

"Happy to complete our family and your wish, ma!" Nandni would say.

" Yes, my daughter," Usha kissed Nandni's forehead. Nandni teared up.

Usha's joy knew no bounds when their family doctor, Dr. Sharma, revealed that Nandni was expecting twins. Usha's feet were uncontrollable. She was frantically gathering local vegetables, fruits, and juices to prepare a meal for Nandni. Nandni, in her mind, required the utmost care because she was responsible for feeding two lives.

The Bhatia residence used to be noisy because of Usha's constant movement between the ground floor and the third floor. Due to the vulnerability of her pregnancy, Nandni chose to stay in the room on the ground floor so that she would not have to climb many stairs to visit her family... The space on the first floor serves as Usha and Ramesh's bedroom as well as her kitchen... On the second floor is a private area for Kunal and Nandni, and the third floor was empty after Kiran's wedding.

It's time to give Nandni her medicine, Mom. Please do so. Kunal's voice could be heard clearly from the second floor, for it was more like a tone of liberty rather than an order.

Yes, I'm going to get some orange juice, and I'll bring the medicine with me... The appointment for her ultrasound is approaching; have you made it yet? Usha raised her voice on the first floor, which allowed it to travel to the second floor and reach Kunal's ears. I've already scheduled an appointment for her. While I wait for her to finish taking her medication, I will take her to the doctor. Kunal, who was on the second floor, replied.

Nandni was treated like a princess by Usha, and she made sure that her every waking moment, hour, and day were taken care of with the utmost attention to detail.

The day was busy as usual for Usha with all her schedules for Nandni. Unless and until another piece of astonishing news stuck in Usha's ears, which turned Usha into a breathing statue. This time it was about Kanchan's pregnancy. Usha was amazed by the one million happening that all her daughters were pregnant simultaneously. Happiness knew no bounds, for it washed each and every stone and brick of the house. Kanchan herself was confused as to where to push over her concentration. She wished to pamper Krishiv and Abeer, care for Nandni and Kiran with her unique effort and style and take care of herself too. Her cravings seemed quite different during her second pregnancy, yet she was lovable. Months rolled by like fast-paced leopard paws.

The clouds parted ways on October 1st, allowing a glorious ray of sunshine to shine brightly into the Tandon's home.

Shanayaa brought light into the house, and everyone in it adored her just as much as they did Usha ki Kiran. An extraordinarily adorable and teeny-tiny little girl with dark brown eyes won over the hearts of her family with each one of her smiles. The cutest moment was when she was sleeping all serene, knowing well that she dawned at the most shielded place in this whole world. Both the kids, Kiran, were like two different versions of her. The heads were barely out of the waters of joy until a piece of news drowned them with the flood of delight.

Usha met Kiran and her new baby thanks to Kunal, who brought her to the hospital.

Tiny hands held Usha's finger as she held her in her arms as if saying, *"I AM YOUR FIRST RAY."* As Usha stands for dawn and Kiran stands for Rays of Light, it was as if little Shanayaa was claiming legal rights for owning both. Both Usha's and Shanayaa's hearts smiled!

Usha started her same routine set of questions with Kiran.

"Kiran, Shanayaa is hungry, I guess. Why is she not stopping her cry? Try feeding her."

"Yes, mom, I did a few minutes back. I think her stomach is upset. Should we consider Dr. Sharma?"

In a few minutes, well-experienced Usha reached her with hand medicine.

"Feed her this after her milk," Usha said. Baby's tears became feeble and vanished in seconds.

Sametime, Nandni was about to finish her seventh month of pregnancy, and Usha was working hard to plan a Baby Shower for her.

"Nandni! look if this saree would suit you!" Usha brought a brand-new saree to Nandni with all her love.

Nandni grabbed the saree, held it close to her chest, and said, "yes... Yes... My favorite color. How did you find it?"

Nandni jumped and hugged Usha. "Thank you, ma... Thank you... "She repeated with tears.

Usha, with sudden anxiety, exclaimed, "No... Nooo... Nandni... You cannot be too fast... Try to be a little gentle."

"Sure ma... "Nandni replied in her childish voice.

Women from the community and friends and family were invited to come together and celebrate the soon-to-be mother and her unborn children while indulging in some delectable treats.

Little Shanayaa was the center of attraction as she sat in Nandni's lap throughout the function. During the event, all the family members prayed for Nandni to bless them with a baby boy and a baby doll, just like Shanayaa. Nandni's due date approached, and due to the complications of carrying twins, Dr. Sharma advised Nandni to have a C-Section for her safer delivery.

Nandni's safety was Usha's top priority. As Nandni was carrying twins, it was difficult for her to move around with her daily chores. She got hungry every 10 minutes, out of her control. She always felt a mild fear hoping both the fetuses were doing healthy. Nandni was scared of walking at the beginning of pregnancy, fearing losing it, for those were the apple of her eyes.

Later, as the baby bump grew, Nandni's body weight grew by 20 kgs.' which was difficult for her to hold. However, constant support from Usha day and night kept her going. Usha used to be the biggest motivator. Nandni may forget her medicines, but Usha was always up to speed to keep the minor details on her tips. With the love and care she received from Usha; Nandni always felt as if she could have been born as a daughter to Usha. But all she could do was thank the stars that paved the way to marry Kunal, which got her a beautiful and robust mother-in-law.

On the auspicious day of Shivratri (an auspicious Hindu festival), Usha and Kunal waited impatiently outside the operating theatre. Finally, the nurse announced it is a girl and a boy. Usha's mind helplessly pondered over Nandni's wellbeing. Despite his eyes shedding tears of joy, Kunal looked at his mother awestruck, wondering about her relationship with his wife.

"How is Nandni doing?" Inquired Usha to the nurse.

Both children and their mother are in good health... hushed the nurse and hurried inside. The girl's 2 minutes older echoed the nurse's voice...

The good news spread quickly, and Usha's phone rang nonstop with congratulations. Though weird, she wished she had millions of hands and ears to hear and embrace those congratulatory words without letting them go in vain.

And the kids and mom came home, and Usha's day got busy taking care of two little ones and her daughter-in-law. There was a discussion about the name to be kept for children, and Kunal asked Usha for her opinion, and she suggested getting the idea of her daughters as well.

Since the kids were born on Shivratri, Kiran suggested that the girl be named *Gauravi,* which is another name for Goddess Parvati which means "honor and pride," and that the boy be named *Gatik,* which is one of Lord Shiva's many names and means "fast, forward." After what seemed like only a blink of an eye, a month had passed when the Nanda's announced the arrival of their second child on Krishiv's birthday. April 7th was marked as the birthday of both the sons of Kanchan.

The little angel was more adorable that even Rahul could express. He was the sweetest little guy that he has ever seen, His super smile stole Nanda's heart, and his hairstyle makes him look like a mini-Kanchan.

Usha was thrilled to learn the news and could hardly wait to meet her new grandson, a miniature version of Kanchan, her favorite daughter. Kanchan's eyes were moist from her happiness, and she embraced her mother and said, "Mom... One more boy in your LAP." No one could have been more fortunate today than Usha; it's six now, and no one could have been more fortunate than me.

She held little Kanchan in her arms, and the little boy with small black eyes and glowing golden skin wearing a blue shirt winked pleasantly as if he was saying hello to his Nani. Kanchan being Lord Krishna's devotee, named him *Kanav,* which means earing of Lord Krishna.

Kanchan was well aware of Usha's routine of making the mother and baby healthy. With little idea of watching Kiran closely during her pregnancies. Kanchan was on track with Usha's queries.

Usha called out. Kanchan!

Before Usha could say another word, Kanchan would say.

"Yes, mom. I bathed early at 5 am and sanitized Kanav's sipper and clothes. Both would burst out with laughter.

****

The Bhatia residence quickly became the neighborhood hot spot. Everyone's hearts used to melt whenever they saw adorable little Gauravi with her brown hair and blue eyes. Wherein the young Krishna (Gatik) of Usha was a delight to his grandparents.

Usha was a bit different for Nandni, for she never questioned her. Instead, she carried out each and every chore for her. Nandni started healing from delivery pressures. Gauravi and Gatik took their steps and began growing.

On the days, when Kiran and Kanchan visit with their children, Usha was overjoyed and had double the amount of responsibility to manage and compromise all her six grandchildren.

Abeer would call out. "Nani... Nani.... Take a look. I've made this out of clay."

Before Usha took hold of it, Krishiv would run in between. "Nani... Take a look at mine. I did it more beautifully than Abeer."

Abeer started Crying. Usha convinced their lovely cry by grading their little creation equally.

"The red one in the small bowl

The little one in the big bowl...". Usha has given instructions to Gauravi, Gatik, Shanayaa and Kanav.

To keep the children occupied, Usha combined kidney beans, chickpeas, and a variety of other lentils, and then she instructed the children to separate the ingredients into separate bowls. During the night, she would sit upright on the bed while requiring the children to sit on her knees. The kids felt like they were going on a fun ride when she started moving her knees, which sparked the following amusement. The giggles and chortles filled the house air, which began to take its course throughout the neighborhood.

Laughter rang out from every corner of the house because they had many toys to play with. The chuckles attracted many souls who found peace by admiring the kids playing with their Nani and Dadi.

Gauravi was extremely beautiful, and she was the peak of pride for Usha. Everyone used to envy her for her beauty. Gauravi received many requests for modelling assignments. Wherein Gatik was a lucky charm of his grandmother, a replica of his father, Kunal. He would steal away anyone's heart with his affectionate nature and good manners, which Usha taught him. His signature statement was to bow his head down to whoever elder comes to the house as a gesture of paying respect. Ramesh and Usha's siblings always praised the beautiful upbringing Usha has done with her grandkids.

It was the time when Gatik and Gauravi were turning one. Usha expressed a desire to celebrate their birthday on a grand scale, inviting all their relatives and friends. An event planner was hired to execute the Mickey Mouse theme in a banquet hall for a fantastic great birthday celebration for children.

Excellent food, lots of games, amazing balloon art decoration, lovely return gifts for the kids, and lots of candies were the party's main attractions.

A lot of people had good things to say about the birthday party, and Usha was overjoyed to hear their well wishes for the children.

****

It was Usha's favorite pastime to play online Ludo with Krishiv and Abeer, the two oldest children in the family. They became the cutest responsible for the fellas that followed them into this earth. Gatik and Gauravi, on the other hand, were occupied with shaping the wheat dough into various utensils and shapes. Once more, Usha was passing on her art and the knowledge she had gained from her Bala Aunty.

On the days when all the children are gathered together, Usha's favorite pastime was to keech between the children by stacking glasses and throwing them a softball which each of the six tried hard to attain.

At around that time, reports began to circulate about a deadly virus taking lives. As a result, Usha did not allow her children to go out and play with other children or go on play dates. Instead, she kept her children confined in her home.

As the calendar year drew close, Kiran hosted a Christmas party at her house and invited Usha, Gatik, and Gauravi to attend. Kiran called out with all her preparations awaiting the guests. She also asked Usha to bring Christmas cookies. The general idea was not complicated at all. Every child will receive a present from each family. On the evening before Christmas, Kiran hosted a party for six different families, which included a total of ten children.

The celebration started with food and taking pictures with a Christmas tree... Then, it was planned for one family member to dress up as Santa Claus and make a surprise appearance in front of the children, at which point they would hand out gifts to the children...

The floor was now open for Usha, the actual Santa of the unified family, not only for her grandkids but also her kids for decades. A Santa Claus of two generations. Grabbing her senses back, she insisted that Kunal dress up as Santa.

While Kunal was acting as Santa Claus and handing out presents to children, it was time for him to give something to his children... Gauravi was happy to receive the gift and danced on the jingle bells. She dragged Usha to call Abeer for her. Dadi... Tell Abeer to dance with me. Usha pulled Gauravi, trying to divert her, come dance with me, my child.

But Gatik was extremely frightened, and this caused everyone else to laugh. Gatik was shocked and uttered, Dadi... I'm afraid. He turned and hugged himself into Usha's saree. When Usha removed Kunal's mask and revealed that it was his father dressed as Santa, she could not stand the thought of Gatik being frightened.

At the party, people voiced their worries which echoed from various nooks and corners, about the virus's potential to spread further from China. And after the party, they went back to their house.

Usha wanted to make sure that none of her daughters had the impression that she spent more time with one of them, so she decided to celebrate the new year with Kanchan and Nanda's family, along with their children. Usha greeted the new year with the same cheer she always does and made plans for her complete body checkup.

Because she was aware of Ramesh's health and that the number of cases of the first wave of COVID-19 was increasing, she decided to stay at home and postpone her tests. She did not want to bring the virus home, as this could risk either Ramesh's health or the health of the young children living in the house.

Chapter

8

An Unwanted Guest

An Unwanted Guest

Something was lurking beneath the thin sheet of skin and a muscle layer inside the bone cage. Why couldn't there be any gadget that allows one to access the insides of a human body with one swipe or click? Never mind the USG (Ultra Sonography) X-Ray machines, more sophisticated X-Ray machine that shoots multiple shots and is called CT or PET, or more sophisticated machine called MRI. How about a camera eye with a bit of light that is as small as the point of a needle? It would be easy to penetrate the needle and watch what's happening inside the troubled area. But with no need for sonography, the daughters could see right through their mother. Though they failed in their attempt to detect the reason for their mother's agony, Kiran and Kanchan caught the guard of their mother, seeping deep down in pain. Mother and her daughters could feel the cold winter-like breeze sticking to their bones for a moment but did not know the reason for their fear. All they could do was advance Usha to go through a thorough examination.

Of late, a sense of discomfort in the abdomen was troubling Usha... COVID-19 had already entered Indian territory dictating enormous fear, horror, and panic. Authorities announced a lockdown, and life came to a standstill. Life and the world got reduced within four walls, and even other creatures cowered securely in their hideouts, sensing a catastrophe.

Usha couldn't go out to a pathological lab to get her blood samples tested. It seemed the entire world was dead and gone as if it had never existed except for the houses and buildings.

The color of Usha's skin was starting to get more yellow. The lockdown was kept in place, but there were occasional, fleeting breaks in its enforcement. Kunal sought medical attention for her, and the doctor from the nearby clinic prescribed medications based on the symptoms.

Kunal didn't waste time getting medicines for Usha and starting her treatment. He couldn't bear the sight of his mother being sick.

"Why is this yellowish complexion not going away?" Nandni asked Kunal out of worry.

"Umm... looks like the medicines are not working...."

Kunal replied to Nandni's question.

"That must be the case. Their prescription might be of hit-or-miss nature.". Nandni replied.

Kunal went to the same doctor; this time, the doctor advised her whole body to be examined...

Kunal scheduled the tests online with a renowned pathology lab. A representative from the lab reported the patient to be on an empty stomach before taking samples...

The next day, Usha got up early because she was nervous about giving her samples. A lab technician came and took blood samples from Usha.

On the terrace in the evening, while Kunal and Usha were having a cup of tea, the screen of Kunal's phone illuminated with a text message. The notification confirmed that the reports from Usha had been delivered successfully.

Kunal went back to his room to check the results on his laptop. As he was doing so, he saw some irregularities in the statistics that were being reported for the liver functioning tests. He contacted Dr. Sharma (retired from the Indian Army) for guidance on the findings.

"Doctor Sir, the whites of my mother's eyes are becoming yellow. I've sent you the results of her full body check-up."

While Kunal was on the phone with him, Dr. Sharma checked the reports that Kunal sent him.

"Undoubtedly, she suffers from a liver condition. I beg you not to waste any time. Take her to the hospital." The sharpness of the statement pierced the inner poles of Kunal's heart, shattering it into pieces.

"Sir.... How can I get her hospitalized, given that every hospital is a Covid Centre?" Kunal replied.

Dr. Sharma, a Nobel laureate and former Army officer, answered, "Let me see what I can do about getting you an appointment at the Institute of Liver and Biliary Sciences. It is a well-known hospital for liver treatment."

As soon as Dr. Sharma offered his assistance, Kunal made haste to get Usha to the hospital so she could obtain medical care.

Kiran and Kanchan joined their brother Kunal in the hospital, where Usha received her treatment. This was a terrible ordeal. Nobody in the family had ever seen her confined to bed before.

"Is it even possible for her to spend the entire day confined to her bed?" " Kiran, who hardly saw her mother sick, asked Kanchan in disbelief.

"There's something very wrong here. Considering how mom has always been active and cared for her health, getting sick to the extent of getting admitted is unbelievable."

Meanwhile, the pandemic remained persistent. It had taken the lives of many people all over the world. India wasn't an exception.

Amidst this miserable situation, Usha's treatment was progressing. After the general tests, there were more specific tests, such as a tissue sample.

The doctors quickly scheduled surgery to implant a stent in Usha's liver so that they could drain the excessive amount of bilirubin that was causing her jaundice.

Except for the times she gave birth to her precious gems Kiran, Kanchan, and Kunal, Usha never was admitted to a hospital, this being her first time since then. Usha was terrified because it had never occurred to her in her strange dreams that she would be undergoing surgery in a hospital. Nevertheless, she submitted to the experience, expecting everything to turn out right.

Kiran, Kanchan, and Kunal were waiting outside the surgery room for their mother to come out...

As soon as the red light in the OT room was turned off, all of the siblings' attention was drawn to the OT room, where the staff members were bringing Usha on a bed...

She was aware of her surroundings but was terrified and could only spell. Kunal...Kunal...

Her eyes were looking for her son, the only person who could save her from the doctors' pain.

When Kiran and Kanchan saw how helpless their mother was, they could barely maintain their composure and could only murmur, "Mom, you will be alright."

Usha slept soundly throughout the night because of her medications. On the other hand, Kunal could not close his eyes even for a second, for his anxiety was eating him alive.

At 10 a.m., the doctors came and asked Kunal to walk out of the room, explaining that jaundice would subside because a stent had been placed in his liver. However, there is more to discuss than just jaundice.

With a puzzled expression, Kunal enquired, "What Doctor?"

Dr. Arora replied, "The test findings are not positive..."

When the doctors verified the diagnosis as cancer of the gallbladder stump that had spread to the liver, it felt like the sky had fallen. "It's possible that she just has six months left to live." Before the doctor could even complete the sentence, Kunal became paralyzed with pain.

Kunal was speechless... and firmly questioned, "How can we save her doctor?".

Dr. Arora replied, "Surgery is out of the question because the disease has gotten too bad. Chemotherapy could be an option, though."

"Will my mother be okay after this?" Kunal inquired.

"Chemotherapy may extend her life by a month or two at most..." The doctor said with reluctance.

To Nandni, Kiran, and Kanchan, Kunal broke the devastating news. The news devastated the entire family and threw them all into a sea of torment. They were all terrified that they might lose Usha...

After consulting with his sisters, Kunal decided that he would not let Usha know that she was harboring a potentially fatal illness inside her body.

Kiran and Kanchan stayed in the hospital on alternate days with Usha to support Kunal.

Usha felt peaceful seeing her daughters visit her in the hospital. Still, she was oblivious that she was harboring a potentially fatal illness within her own body.

The news spread like wildfire once it got out. Nobody ever had any reason to suspect. Cancer is not contagious nor passed down through families. Medical professionals are of this opinion. However, after Usha was diagnosed with cancer at stage 3, the family started having second thoughts about the reliability of medical knowledge. It felt like a fistful of sand falling through fingers like sand through a sieve. That's how it appeared at the time. Everyone, including the health professionals, felt utterly powerless.

It was precisely the same as the day before; Usha was hurrying about as usual. There were no outward manifestations of any illness. Perhaps she was aware of the warnings but chose to ignore them, just as many of us do. She never mentioned any symptoms or the agony she was experiencing. Who stated, "Ignorance is bliss?" and why? It seemed like a curse.

The siblings got together to debate whether or not the diagnosis was accurate. Normally, our brain has a negative bias, but in these situations, the negative bias operates in the opposite direction. Nobody was willing to admit that the medical doctors were correct in their assessment. Instead, self-denial slowly sprouted its stubborn branches inside everyone's minds, blinding them to the ugly truth.

In the meantime, all of Usha's family members and friends called Kunal and Nandni to inquire about Usha's health and expressed their willingness to pay a visit to her while in the hospital.

They were more thoughtful and caring. However, due to the increased number of COVID cases, Kunal had respectfully suggested that friends and family members refrain from visiting to reduce the risk of infection to his mother.

The efforts of Usha's family to discover an alternative treatment for her illness kept them very busy. They were doing internet surfing tirelessly, looking for a way out... The families of people who had previously been affected by diseases of a similar nature were contacted. The search engines were crawling with oncologists and other practitioners of alternative medicine, as well as specialists and quacks. While everyone else was frantically looking for ways to help her, Kunal was busy finding a solution to her predicament.

Kunal considered sitting by her side, trying to comprehend the trauma she had never spoken about.

A few diagnostic procedures were required before the potentially fatal illness could be established, but the results were precise. Kunal felt it was vital to study and comprehend his previous life and his new life following the event. He was not a research scholar and did not work in the scientific field. He was neither a medical doctor nor an emergency medical technician. His main concern was how it was even possible for Usha to have progressed to the third stage of gallbladder cancer while he was completely unaware of it.

His concern was that medical science could not recognize signs that could save lives.

Kunal made it his purpose to be there for Usha, listen to her woes, and inquire subtly about how she has been experiencing a shift in her emotions. He was interested in learning what she had been thinking for the past year or more. He was curious whether he or anyone else in the family had, on purpose, disregarded sure warning signs or symptoms.

Mothers are known for their nurturing and sentimental nature. They work nonstop until they are so exhausted that they can no longer stand. They give their lives for the sake of their families, but their families do not share their lives with them.

Kunal vowed to devote his life to her. They put in a lot of effort to cover up the term 'cancer' from the elderly. It was more like a cursed treasure that needed utmost protection deep under the ocean where Ramesh and Usha can never reach as cancer, a name in itself can give a heart attack.

He was spending more time in the hospital, so he could listen to Usha talk about how she felt.

The hospital room was well-lit, tidy, and clean. There was a bed that was the size of a king right in the middle.

"Ever since I was a child, I have spent most of my life fighting against a wide variety of challenges, some of which have been illnesses. I have never been paranoid. I did not have the opportunity to reflect on the state of my physique." Usha to Kunal

Usha sat up in bed and stretched her legs out. Usha gave off the appearance of being somewhat fragile and exhausted, and anxious. She was unaware of the actual situation. She was informed that the condition was not fatal and that it could be treated. There was never a single mention of the word "cancer."

Kunal was delving into her recent medical history. This was a complex scenario. He didn't want to come out as worried or curious. But he was keen to hear what had happened in the previous year. So, he decided it would be best to talk about her aunt, who had died a year previously. Usha was close to her aunt, and he thought it would be an excellent place to start digging a little further. He inquired. "Did you know anything about your aunt's health six months before she died?"

"We've known each other since I was a kid and always bonded through our shared interests. With her around, my childhood was filled with interesting events. We learned how to be tenacious, tough, and resilient. Pain, pains, fever, and other minor health conditions were rarely taken seriously in our society." Usha took a few deep breaths and then continued. She glanced at the floor before turning away her focus from the ceiling.

Her right hand reached out to hold Kunal's.
He offered it wholly.

She grasped his hand and exhaled deeply, looking at his eyes. She did not forget the subject or the final sentence. That was incredible.

"We either disregard these pains because we've learned to live with them, or we accept them. We also practiced self-medication. If that doesn't work, we'll just go to the nearest pharmacy and ask for the medication without being diagnosed or treated by a doctor. The chemist would not charge a consultation fee and would occasionally provide medicine on credit. This was the norm where I grew up." Her lips gave in a hollow smile...

As she closed her eyes, she inhaled a sigh of relief. Retracting from Kunal's hands, she caressed her cheeks and smiled. She shifted her weight and hung her legs off the edge of her bed. For someone her size, the bed was a bit too high. She turned her weight to the edge of the bed, allowing her feet to rest on the floor. The hot weather made the tiled floor feel a little chilly. She longed to touch the ground.

Both of Kunal's hands were nestled between hers.

Kunal could feel her gentle and caring fingertips. They were pals.

Maybe she, too, wanted to locate herself next to someone with whom she felt appeased. But, despite her best efforts, Kunal's hand was melting down from her clench.

Kunal capitulated. Once more, he raised his gaze to her. When she was done, he sat back and waited. Also, she was aware that he was genuinely interested in hearing her saga.

"There are lots of people, cars, and shops in Paharganj.

People are always talking, vendors are hollering, cars are honking, and sometimes there are fights and people are yelling. From the outside, it was too much to bear. But it was our only way to stay alive. After midnight, I would sometimes suddenly wake up and hear nothing. Then I felt like I had landed in a cemetery. Paharganj was so quiet that it sounded like death. Paharganj was always lively." Usha's smile brightened up her face.

Kunal thought she had already dived into the past that had the most serious effect on the vast and crystal-clear ocean. She seemed to be trying to remember some great times when she was swimming with her utmost might and passion by looking up. Kunal put out his right hand and took hold of hers with it.

He inquired... "You must have seen a variety of persons in that place?"

Her lips were extended as she smiled broadly.

"We've always referred to Paharganj as a small world and a miniature India. There were always white and dark-skinned foreigners wandering around. There were individuals from all religions and areas of India present. They all spoke in their native tongues. It was difficult to keep track of many languages, but I enjoyed listening to them. There were also a lot of touts and travel agencies chasing these tourists down to sell the tours and travel packages. I often considered turning my house into a motel for these visitors. They were decent individuals. I did not encounter a single individual who was furious or anxious. These visitors from wealthy and developed countries liked their stay in Paharganj. I was perplexed as to why there were no tension marks on their faces. Perhaps the stress and anxiety were intended for Indians who live in highly populated areas." Her expression darkened suddenly like the sun surrounded by dark clouds with no warning.

Kunal did not let her fall into this predicament. He was eager to learn more. He softly caressed her hands and rose from his seat to sit next to her. He urged her to sit on the hard bed with her legs crossed so he could do the same. She didn't say anything but quietly hosted a profound calculation deep within.

When Usha flexed her knees, she shifted them outwards, making her legs appear longer. It was as though she had placed one foot on top of another. He was observant of her behavior. However, he was able to sit cross-legged on the ground. She gave him a tip. She said, "move your weight on your hips rather than your feet. When sitting on the floor, position your tummy over your hips. Take a cushion or a blanket to put beneath your knees if you're uncomfortable or feel pressure on your hips."

She grabbed a nearby cushion and threw it under Kunal's right knee to make him more comfortable.

He did not resist. He wanted to know more, even if he had to stay up all night without eating or drinking. Usha was in the mood to talk for a long time. He didn't want to interrupt what she was thinking.

She began to speak.

"You might think I'm petrified inside but talking to you makes me feel much better. I'd like to let you know that I'm a winner. I'm not scared of these diseases. The death of my father shook me to my core. Your dad has been sick for quite a while. Nothing has the power to shake me."

"People are being ignorant, knowing well that it'll help them less. They fear poverty, hardship, and suffering. "I believe these are a part of our lives." Usha hesitated for a moment. She stared up as if looking for stars that speak louder than the still moon in a deep-seated sheet of a dark night. It was in vain as her sight got blocked by the hospital room's ceiling. There weren't any.

Her search for something seemed a bit odd to Kunal. Despite this, she kept staring at the ceiling as if her eyes could break through the concrete and gaze at the sky. Usha inhaled deeply and fixed her gaze on Kunal's face. He noticed her maturing into a philosopher. Even though her white eyes were yellow, her eyes shone. In his mind, he imagined she heard voices from the supernatural. She regained her composure and began speaking again.

"When God made the first person, He gave him intelligence, freedom of choice, and the ability to suffer. We get all of that. He also said he would help if there were trouble. We abuse our freedom of choice. We don't make good use of our minds. Everyone wants money, comfort, and power. No one says they'd be happy with a low-paying job and a simple but meaningful life. When Adam and Eve left heaven, a dog named "ego" went with them. We also refer to it as the devil or Satan. We don't try to see God everywhere, but our ego is always behind us. The more you get ahead in life and try to get rich, the bigger this dog gets going hand in hand with its huge waving foxlike tail. However, they never seem to expand their thinking beyond its current confines.

Kunal had never witnessed Usha, the philosopher, or the philosopher within her. Never before..."

Honestly! He believed a Ph. D. was not required to be a philosopher. Usha was directly in front of him with the imaginary mortarboard hat that Kunal presented her with.

The countdown to death had begun for the woman, but she was unaware of it. She was referring to God the Father. When she was younger, she seemed to be a knowledgeable person. It's hard to imagine how someone could do that. How, exactly, can a woman do this in a male-dominated world? This is a bit out of character. It's mind-boggling to see something like this. Usha? Who was the Paharganj woman? A woman exposed to the harsh realities of poverty, discomfort, and humility.

What's going on?... Kunal pondered over with the question. Because of our youth, we believe that previous generations, such as those of Gen X', the Baby Boomers, and others who have long since faded from our consciousness, have no idea what they're talking about. Most of us have forgotten how we got our genes. We carry their DNA and inherit what they teach us. The intellect and other traits that used to define Usha must have been sacrificed for her to have children.

Usha paused for a moment's peace. She asked Kunal to drink and eat something. The staple food of the Punjabi community is paratha and saag, or everything that goes with paratha. Paratha can be made plain or stuffed with potatoes, cauliflower, onions, or cottage cheese, depending on one's preference. That's why she requested two Parathas from the hospital kitchen for Kunal.

Kunal climbed out of the sofa and went to the bathroom.

He sat in the western-style ceramic water closet for about ten minutes in the restroom. The washroom had a wonderful aroma depicting the vibes that the hospital room attained from Usha despite her ailment.

The focus of his attention was solely on Usha. He'd never known her so intimately in his entire life. She spoke with power and fluency. It was a life-changing encounter. He had underestimated the importance of homemakers. After a while, he began questioning whether Usha was indeed an extrovert or just an enigma. Did she know her capabilities?

Meanwhile, ten minutes went by. After washing his hands and face, he stood up and walked out. He pulled the chair out and sat down for the second time. A young girl from the Hospital pantry's support staff entered the room with a large tray of food. He caught a whiff of hot, fresh paratha. In Kunal's mind, he wanted to jump and eat as soon as the tray was placed on the table.

Pickles of two varieties surprised him. Keralan mixed and olive pickle. This came as such a shock. Olive pickles were new to him. A little steel bowl of curd sat in one of the tray's corners. Freshly produced butter was found in a third bowl. The food looked good. For a split second, Kunal lost sight of why he was with Usha in the first place. It was still one paratha with pickles and curd that he consumed. However, he required much more energy to hear and gather rest from Usha. The girl gave Usha a bowl of soup.

Their conversation veered, of course, and turned to topics like family and friends. Kunal longed to hear more. He was on the lookout for a way to take her back to a time in her recent past. He was eager to learn about her history and whether or not she had experienced any cancer signs.

The girl who brought the food returned with a cup of tea in her hand. She cleaned the table, and Kunal got busy with Usha, the daughter of heaven. Her name was apt. Her personality went well with what her name meant. He didn't move from his seat and asked her to stretch her legs. She knew that he was waiting for her to tell the following narrative.

Usha returned to where she had left the treads and gathered them in a moment to start knitting again. She had a great memory. Even though she was in her 60s, she could remember the last thing she said almost an hour ago. She leaned back and put her back on the queen-size soft brown fabric backrest that looked like leather. Kunal wondered if brown was her favorite color or if it was just a chance thing. He didn't want to ask and take her mind off something else. She twisted her head to the left and right as if working out her neck muscles.

Usha explained why she kept turning her head from left to right. "I haven't been feeling good for a long time. I don't know if my stiff neck is because of my pillow or how I sleep. I tried to switch pillows. It's not a big deal, though. I sometimes have pain in the upper part of my stomach, right below my ribcage. I didn't tell anyone how bad it hurt. I don't want people to worry about me. I went through hard times as a child. It was hard to get by. We were all so used to anxiety, pain, and aches because we had lived with them all our lives. Whenever my life was calm for a few days, I felt strange. All that comfort, solace, and peace was so short-lived and strange to us. The truth is that I was scared after a few days of living without any problems. I knew that something bad was about to happen when the sea was quiet. We have grown up worrying, sadness, pain, and not knowing what will happen. All of them were our friends and family. I didn't feel whole without these problems. Usha took a deep breath and held it as long as she could as if her thoughts so far might escape her with one blow. Then cautiously, she let out a breath and went on.

"Sometimes I wish I could turn back the clock and return to those times." There were good and awful times. But then I remember the horrible moments. I had their loyalty. I shall lose the meaning of perseverance if I eliminate them from my past. I will likewise be unable to comprehend emotional empathy. Those "difficult days" taught me how to share. Everything but trauma, pain, and discomfort should be shared. Share in the anguish, sadness, and annoyance of others. Do you know that I was the main man of the house in my father's absence?? Yes! That is correct. Let me tell you about one of the most important things my father ever taught me. Listen carefully and pay attention."

With pride, Usha lifted her brows. She shifted her posture in her chair. Usha sat back down and resumed her conversation. She had a smile on her face. She had something to say that made her feel proud of her father. "My father taught me how to capitalize," she claimed. When we were all there in our modest house one day. Catching a rubber ball my father intended to throw at me, he instructed. He picked a ball and threw it at me in a flash. My nose bled when the ball struck it. Everybody in the house was in disbelief at the news.

I don't understand why he did this to me. It was clear to me that it was not a form of punishment. You didn't look at the ball when I threw it, he added, but at my hand and me instead. It was your fault. When you didn't see the target, you were hit. After I had regained my composure, he took up the ball again and told me to keep my eyes firmly fixed on the ball. I was able to catch the ball this time when he threw it. Nothing in school or from a teacher ever taught me this lesson. An essential part of the exercise was educating me on how to concentrate on a specific object, person, or circumstance. As a result of his guidance, I've become an expert."

Usha waited for Kunal's words of praise for her father. His head fell in reverence. He couldn't put into words what his grandfather had taught his mother. Everything is blown out of proportion in the digital age. We make poor use of the resources available due to their low cost and accessibility. Digital Landscape is a bargain. Similar abilities in teaching children would be showcased in an online webinar or YouTube video. This is achievable with so many degrees, years of expertise, and readily available resources. Usha's father lacked financial means. A man who rode his bicycle to work and home every day for half his life, despite the bad weather, to provide for his family. The best teaching practice was this excellent way of explaining the notion of "concentration" to the home audience.

The door was slammed open by a knock. Kunal then realized that it was visiting hours and Kanchan and Rahul arrived. After a long wait, Usha was delighted to see her daughter and son-in-law come.

Kunal was miffed. The situation appeared to be ideal. Usha was in a good mood and was eager to talk about her past and recent experiences. On Kunal's face, she said: "Don't worry, we will continue in a short time. Let me now spend some time with your sister and brother-in-law.

All the while she was in the hospital, she took good care of everyone. Without words to express himself, Kunal left the second-floor lobby and went outside.

While he was sipping his coffee, Kunal reminisced about his recent encounter with Usha. It brought back memories of the day he had spent on their roof top a few months before.

His patio had always been a favorite set down for him. It was covered up. The terrace was a perfect size, six feet wide and ten feet long. On the terrace, there were two chairs. He remembered Usha's fondness for the color brown as he remembered the chair. Resilience and security are associated with the color's earthy hue. It seemed quite probable that she advanced a taste for the color brown due to her difficult upbringing. In his mind, she was a patient like the earth, which he likened to her. She possessed a level of resiliency that was unparalleled.

A shift in the sun's position had taken place. He was the only one in the hospital corridor wandering without being aware that he might be an unwelcome guest for many gloomy impulses. In the lobby, people were less concerned about the soul, which had been infected by a dreadful sickness and would only have a limited time left in the human world, than they were.

No one could perceive Usha in that situation. Kunal's eyes were a little teary. He made his way to the parking lot and gazed at the sky.

"Why are you so ruthless?" he begged the almighty.

A few tears streamed down his cheeks. He wished he could return to his school days. He would study human anatomy. He desired to become a doctor with a mission. He would research oncology and treat all of the world's maladies. He'd strive to give them a second chance at life. More tears streamed down his cheeks. He was wiping his tears away when he felt a light touch on his right shoulder. It somehow felt like a mild yet intense stinge from a bee that had been disturbed by its meditation. When he turned around, Kanchan stood behind him and informed him that Usha was looking for him. Kunal returned to his hospital room.

Kunal was in the mood to find out more, so he asked her about her health in the past few months. With her two hands, Usha cradled Kunal's face and whispered, "take it easy. This isn't a big deal. We were taught self-help techniques. I've always felt delighted to accomplish things for my family and others. In my father's absence, I was the main man of the home, as I already stated. It is now tough for your generation or the generation after you. There was a time when people enslaved people. However, the era of slavery has passed. But we have not broken free from that mould. We like to spend money and have everything delivered to our door in today's digital age. We should ideally stroll a few hundred yards to get what we need. Those that do so either drives a car or ride a motorcycle. Requesting that items be brought to your home is helpful for individuals who cannot leave the house for various reasons. Still, it has also become a regular healthy practice. This is also considered slavery. Consider the person who delivers the products. I enjoy doing my work. It may need trekking for miles up and down. But "I like it."

As Usha took a pause, Kunal took the chance to ask her why she hadn't been going out as much lately. He knew this was the right time to ask and that she would answer the way he wanted. He could also dig around more. She resumed talk.

"For the past year or so, I've felt like myself again. While I can't recall exactly when it happened, I do recall feeling a lump in my stomach. The lump bothered me since I assumed it resulted from digestive system "gases" or an airlock. I stayed hungry to eliminate the feeling, but it didn't go away. We're not serious, unfortunately. We tend to overlook our health and the resulting issues. That, in my opinion, is a grave aberration. I remember waking up one morning and finding that the lump had vanished. The following evening, though, I was shivering, and my body temperature was oddly high. I was chilled. I was baffled as to why this was happening. It was during Monsoon. Possibly in the August. It didn't bother me. I was shivering the next night since my body temperature had risen. Someone suggested that an infection could be the cause of the problem. Infection means taking harmful medications. Medicine is something I've always avoided. The only way to deal with the disorder was to ignore them. On the third day, I felt more upbeat. After a week, I noticed a burning feeling when I went to the bathroom in the morning. It was a pale shade of yellow. I had not taken any medication. Even though I drank a lot of water, I couldn't figure out why my urine was yellow. Also, my poop was an unnatural shade of yellow the next day. That made me feel anxious. A rash had begun its advance on my body, and I felt irritated. It wasn't the heat, I'm certain of it. It was November by this point, and the weather had improved considerably. My stomach ailment reappeared. It stayed there for a few days. My apologies if I didn't tell you or seek medical advice. How could I or anybody else in the vicinity have known what was happening? On the other hand, these symptoms were a game of hide-and-seek for me. As far as I was concerned, I entrusted these health difficulties to God and my body." Usha paused in her ramblings.

Kunal was baffled as to why.

He was curious whether or not she'd heard anything concerning her illness. Then he realized it was not possible. Nothing could have been further from the reality for her than what she had always been told. Everyone was under strict orders not to bring up the illness.

Usha got quiet. As far as Kunal was concerned, there was nothing more he could do. He wished she had shared these symptoms with him or sought medical attention. He battled with anger and frustration within himself for his mom's unprofound behavior and his petty ignorance for the past year. In the past year, she would have been in the early stages of the disease. It was possible to treat.

He wondered who was to blame for everything. People, culture, and politics all have a role in shaping a person's perspective. The story of Usha, a 64-year-old iron lady of the Bhatia's, is not new. Cognitive empathy is lacking in us. Life isn't worth anything to us. Too many things could go wrong if we don't take more care. The country, as well as its authorities, must evolve. A positive behavior shift in behavior is required of each of us. If we adopt a scientific mindset, we can extend our lives using common sense.

One thing is sure: he will evolve. He is the one who will bring about a shift in my household and have an impact on others. That is how Usha will live for a long time.

On the other hand, after conducting extensive research on alternative treatments, Kiran shared the reports she had compiled with a few ayurvedic hospitals. One Ayurvedic hospital in Punjab confirmed that Usha could be treated and that they were willing to send the medicines by courier because of the COVID.

This news has brought peace to the family like a mild rainbow that just arrived after a burdensome monsoon, giving them hope that Usha will live a long life.

It appeared to positively affect Kunal's countenance, and he cryptically conveyed to Usha that they had discovered an ayurvedic treatment that could cure her illness and that the treatment would start as soon as she returned home.

Usha's eyes lit up with a gleam as she contemplated that the hospital and the surrounding area would finally be causing her less worry. A lengthy stay in the hospital ended with Usha's discharge, and doctors recommended that she start chemotherapy. After completing the papers, Kunal asked Kiran to drive mom home while he purchased all of her medication. As soon as possible, he wanted his mother to stay home with him instead of in a hospital.

This unwanted guest, cancer, had changed their lives forever and stirred them to the core.

Chapter

9

The Last Battle

The Last Battle

The brightly lit sky betrayed no emotions and reflected its existence as it had for aeons. The birds flew to their destination, some wanting to pamper their chicks and some embracing the arrival of night, unmindful of the circumstance unfolding on land. Kiran Garden was resplendent again with the return of its exquisite Queen, and the locality was humming with sighs of relief. Kunal had ensured that the house was ready to receive his mother with its best foot forward.

"My mother will never face any problem."

The youngest has always been the closest to his mother, notwithstanding the fact the parents and Kunal lived together. Maybe this universe designed points to be unequivocal for it could administer the walking feet and scrolling tongues.

"My son has always been a giver. The love and affection he keeps spreading all around bring a smile to everyone. The more I talk about how much care he takes care of us oldies, the less it would be." Usha would boast in front of her friends, and they would nod appreciatively.

The bespectacled wiry lad, standing at almost 5 feet 9 inches, had a great inclination toward the almighty and the celestial. He had also done a crash course on horoscopes to better understand the play of the planets and their influence on the human edifice.

Kunal was an example that most would provide while expressing one's love for their parents. He had decided to wholeheartedly get his mother back on her feet and not concentrate on work.

Kunal, Nandni, and their twins formed a strong team based on love and affection, and even though Kunal never gave importance to money, the family was well provided for.

The son was strong-willed and wanted to explore every option to save his mother. If that meant greater dependence on the almighty, then so be it.

Ramesh greeted his partner while she entered her abode.

"There is my champion returning to her stadium. Welcome back. Now all that remains is to quickly get well and become the Usha we all know."

"She remains the same. Not a single morsel of energy is lost. All it would take is a few days of rest, and everything would be fine again."

"And that is what we all are looking forward to."

The hearty laughter of Ramesh reverberates across the ground floor. He hadn't laughed so hard for a long time.

She had been away from home for some time, which seemed an eternity to the man. They had seldom lived apart other than the occasional travelling on family occasions. Ramesh had never expressed it, but there was certain helplessness with his wife not around. He, too, had been not keeping well for years now. His health undergoes ebbs and troughs, and today it seemed to be on a high, seeing his wife gingerly entering her refuge.

With a broad smile, he held her hands while she mustered enough energy to paint her face with one too.

Usha went upstairs, towards the first floor. Kunal had envisaged this would be her bedroom for the rest of her days. The house had steep stairs, and he didn't want his mother to travel any further upstairs.

Gauravi and Gatik were excited to have their grandmother back. Usha's life, too, revolved around her grandchildren. They would spend the maximum time with her while she would make merry in their presence.

"Bhatia residence" resonated with the din of children after a long time. The house had fallen silent because of the senior lady's absence. But she was back and wanted to keep no stones unturned to return to the average days. Her charisma alone was capable of inspiriting the whole household.

The kids hugged her and wouldn't let her go. Finally, they insisted that she come upstairs with them, but Kunal would have nothing of it. Usha was to remain on the first floor, and that was final. It was challenging to convince Kunal of matters he had already decided upon. That was not to say that he wasn't flexible. He was, but today wasn't the day.

As the evening progressed and the sky turned dark, the locality sprung into life as its inhabitants started returning from work.

The ground floor had an open layout with a single room

with an attached bathroom. This was Ramesh's domicile. He had become a shadow of his former self and was advised of minimal mobility on stairs. He lived here even during Usha's suffering, though his heart lay elsewhere. The idea behind keeping two eternal lovebirds away from each other while they suffered both physically and emotionally had no justification. But then, when has fate ever had one?

"Dadi, why don't you come up." Gatik would vehemently debate the consequences of his grandmother travelling to another floor. Kunal sternly looked at his son, though the father would rarely raise his voice. He understood the pain of seeing both the child and his grandmother being kept apart. The son cried within, but Usha had to be provided with all the comfort. She was also blissfully unaware of the extent to of the disease ravaged her. It continued while medical science made futile attempts to stop or slow it down.

Like the entire Bhatia residence, the second floor was symmetrical in construction. The passageway, the bedroom, and the hall were aligned similarly to the other floors.

Usha had always dreamt of the second floor. The attached kitchen with all the amenities was the focal point of most activities. The second floor was always teeming with people. Usha loved to entertain guests, and the said floor would be a beehive of laughter and memories.

Kunal and Nandni had ensured that the entire first floor was adequately sanitized. However, they didn't want to take any chances with Usha being in such precarious health. The pandemic was showing no signs of slowing down and preventing secondary infection in such times was the family's sole focus.

"I want to go to the second floor. My heart yearns for it," Usha finally spoke up.

Kunal knew this was coming and, as a precautionary measure, had sanitized the second floor too. The bedroom on that floor was ready, but the son ardently wanted his mother to avoid much stress. Usha wanted to be with her grandchildren and compensate for the lost time. Kunal and Nandni didn't have the heart to respond to this. Nandni has always looked up to her mother-in-law as a woman of substance who wouldn't bow down to circumstances. She was also a lady of few needs and wants, and this was one of the few favors she wanted.

They, too, didn't want their children to stay away from their grandmother, who was back from a stay at the hospital. Also, time was of the essence. Kunal's and Nandni's hearts would break every time they realized it, but they remained stoic in the face of adversity. Usha wasn't supposed to have an inkling of an idea of what befell her. The sadness of losing her would wane in front of seeing her struggle to accept fate helplessly.

The second-floor bedroom welcomed its guest for a long and Usha was the happiest. The sky, too, seemed to reciprocate the feeling as it turned crimson red in the evening. It was nature's way of saying, "have fun," to its enthralled audience.

"Mom, how are you?"

"You finally got the time?"

"But I did come the day before yesterday."

"And yesterday?"

Kanchan lived nearby and was a regular at the "Bhatia

residence." She also shared one of the closest bonds with her mother. Kanchan and Usha's conversation went beyond the usual mother and daughter banter. It was a heady concoction of gossip, sentimentalities, and rants. Both would vent their feelings to each other. The conversation would meander through numerous timelines and milestones and end up with a tight hug. Usha was always looking forward to Kanchan coming over for a quick chat. However, that was not to be on all the days. She mostly made it up by calling her mother three to four times a day, mostly video calling. Marvel of technology the smartphone is. The ubiquitous device has been able to shorten the distance between places and people. One can get connected in a matter of seconds, but somehow it fails to connect souls. It sounds like the network is always futile in such aspects.

Kiran used to visit once a month. She lived the farthest, and her hectic professional life didn't allow her much leeway. Usha knew Kiran's frenetic existence and appreciated the hard work her elder daughter was putting in.

"Hope you eat on time?" Usha would enquire every time Kiran met her.

"Yes, Mom." Kiran would wistfully reply.

She knew that soon this question would never be asked again, and no matter how tightly she held on to it, it had to be let go sooner than later.

Kiran wouldn't indulge in the same banter as Kanchan. The eldest daughter has always been the reticent one. Unlike the garrulous Kanchan, Kiran was ever reserved, somber, and aloof. She would mostly have work-related thoughts constantly playing at the back of her mind. She was also possessive of her parents but never expressed it. Kiran always knew they were under the able umbrella of Kunal, and he would do anything and everything to protect them. The younger brother's dedication towards their parents was something to be seen to be believed, and the sisters were always in awe of it. They also knew that Kunal would be hit the hardest once they left.

"Mom, Kiran has come," Kanchan announced loudly.

"When did you come?" Kiran asked her younger sister.

"Half an hour."

"All right."

Today was the last weekend before Usha's birthday, and since it was on a weekday, impossible for both daughters to attend, they came over to meet her.

"Happy birthday, in advance." The sisters greeted Usha in unison.

"What is advance? Happy birthday. One needs to be present on that day." Kunal was jovially sarcastic in his tone. He would often rib his sisters and never lose an opportunity to throw humor at them.

"It's a working day, and also, Kids have their school," Kiran would respond.

"Forget about him. Tell me how's everyone at home. How are your mother-in-law and Vineet?"

"Everyone is good; Mom and Kids remember you a lot."

"Why don't you get Abeer and Shanayaa to meet me? Then, the Queen will have opportunities to catwalk towards her."

Another Salvo from Kunal was fired.

"What stops you, Sister?"

And they would all laugh in unison.

It was a hearty sight to see the family laughing and making merry together. Ramesh would miss out at times since he was mostly confined to its ground floor room, but Usha would ask Kunal to help his father walk up the stairs so the two partners could see each other. The couple would mostly sit in silence, not uttering a single word, and Ramesh, as his wont, might even start snoring sitting beside her. Usha loved all of it. The silence of him, the noise of him. Her entire life revolved around her husband and their children and grandchildren. She was also a tad worried about her sudden liver condition. She feared she might have to clutch up her feathers and give up on most family activities and dreaded the limitations the doctors might impose on her. But, to her surprise, there were none. The basic Covid precautions apart, there weren't many limitations imposed on her. Yes, the diet did change, and the number of medicines prescribed radically increased, but Usha knew this was all for a good cause.

"Happy Birthday," they all sang together. Even Ramesh was clapping and singing hard that day. His beloved wife was fighting a hard battle, even though she never knew it. Ramesh did worry for her, but today he would celebrate and pray for her long life.

****

Kunal had discovered the beautiful effects of Ayurveda. He had researched hard to find out centres that administered the best Ayurvedic medicines. There was a marked improvement in Usha, and she was almost back to her original self within 15 days of return from the hospital. The downside to cancer treatment by Ayurveda was the amount of medication one must take daily. It was no different for her. 40 tablets and a lot of "Tulsi ark." (Holy Basil Water) Kunal would make sure his mother never missed a single dose.

Usha's youngest child was adamant. Like every loving and dutiful son, he, too, wanted to end his mother's suffering and went deep into the philosophies of alternate medicines. He imagined that the cure for cancer lay somewhere there and swam to the farthest reaches hoping that it would also be found. There was rabid desperation that led to the manic search. Kunal was blind with obstinacy, and rightly so.

The helplessness was palpable, for it scratched his bones deep, and his brain was determined and reckless.

It was August, the month of festivities. Usha wanted to celebrate all of them with enthusiasm.

"Don't want to leave a stone unturned," she retorted confidently.

Every *Raksha Bandhan*[81] Usha would visit her brother's place to tie the Rakhi. However, the children advised her not to venture out with the virus looming menacingly. So, the daughters came over for a grand family get-together. Kunal volunteered to take the sweets and the thread to Usha's brother's house.

---

81 A Hindu festival.

"May you get a long life," the sister's prayed for their young brother. He wryly smiled; his thoughts heavy with the aftermath of his mother's fight against cancer. The happy façade tried impossibly hard to hide the hopelessness within. The pandemic added to the fray, and everyone was on tenterhooks. Protecting Usha from the virus was of paramount concern, and this did cause peculiar challenges for all.

"When are you taking her for the next check-up?" Both Kiran and Kanchan would enquire with Kunal. The son was adamant that it was not at all conducive for her to leave home right now. The clinics were all hotbeds of the disease, and it would be a dangerous proposition to admit Usha anywhere. He was able to persuade his sisters, but the disbelief persisted. The progress of cancer needed a thorough and detailed investigation at a regular layoff. The sudden enhancement due to Ayurveda was heartening for all, but it had to be medically proven. The blind thrust that Kunal was increasingly putting on faith and the entire celestial ecosystem surrounding it was a tad disconcerting. The sisters felt it could be a case of extreme circumstances and the measures one takes to overcome them.

August rolled on, though the Bhatia would look forward to it as "Saawan ka mahina". (The fourth month of the Hindu year begins in late July from the first day of the full moon and ends in the third week of August, the day of the next full moon.)

Navratri, Karwa Chauth, Dussehra, and Diwali marked the festive fervors' end. Usha was always a leader when it came to celebrating the festivals with aplomb and gaiety. The children were worried that it might make their mother uncomfortable, but the days passed uneventfully. Usha also wanted to start having her favorite street foods, but that was a strict no from her children. Not just because of the pandemic but also her condition, which is remained blissfully unaware of. Usha's elder brother and sister-in-law were frequent visitors, but given the times, their visits had dwindled. Usha would reminisce about the times they would spend hours talking and gossiping about the world.

"You know what happened...? It would be her favorite starting salvo. The group of three would roar into laughter amidst a constant flow of food and trivialities. Kunal and Nandni would, at times, stand in the corner and watch them in their little utopia. Most of the discussion wouldn't have any relevance to them, but the hearty cheer and the full-throated giggling couldn't be missed. As the clock kept ticking, one knew these moments would someday be lost forever. Could these be saved in snaps, writings, or sayings? Will that suffice? The conversations would echo against the walls, and those would return as memories amidst the silent future. "Bhatia Residence" was a melting pot of visitors, and their tales and helming were Usha and her infectious affability.

Ayurveda came with a lot of restrictions. There was a blanket ban on citrus fruits and sweets. These were precautions one had to take for the medicines to work. Given the sensitivity of alternate medicines, Kunal and Nandni were extremely careful with Usha's diet.

"Mom, you need to get well quick, after which the entire family goes for a chat walk" (Go out to eat street food), Nandni would assure her mother-in-law.

"And the virus?" the senior lady would retort.

"It too would have a *chat* (street food) with us."

And both would burst into laughter.

The Centre sending the medicines was particular about the patient's diet. They had warned that it would work only if a proper lifestyle was maintained, including stringent food habits. Usha was never a stickler when it came to her eating habits. Her disciplined life was balanced by her love for street food, which she craved for. Her children knew her affinity for the junk but the pandemic and the dreaded disease lurking inside of her were dampeners. Nandni's constant struggle to keep her mother-in-law's spirit in the highest order was appreciable. Last Sunday, Usha almost begged her son to get her chole-kulche (Chickpea curry and A small, round Indian bread made from flour, milk, and butter, typically stuffed with meat or vegetables) but was flatly denied. It broke their hearts for disparate reasons, but the cause was genuine. Someone's feast is indeed someone's poison, and Usha's predicament perfectly fits the bill. Kunal remembers how, each time he would return from work, his hands would be filled with street food for Usha and Ramesh. Both were gastronomes and showed no signs of slowing down even with the passage of time and advancing age., though Ramesh had only recently mellowed down because of his ill health.

"Bring for your mother. My digestion isn't as good as it used to be," Ramesh would rue. However, he would participate in the feast by discussing his past gastronomic valour acts.

"Nandni, why aren't people coming over to me? Hope they know that I exist too," Usha enquired. Nandni was busy dusting the shelf.

"It's been a long time since I have met people." She continued

Nandni continued dusting in silence. She did not have an answer to that and pretended as if the noise of the duster drowned the 65 years old elderly lady's voice. At times pretense is vital. Silence has its beauty, and Nandni used it well. Usha's children have been requesting relatives and closed ones to avoid coming to their place at present due to the prevailing pandemic. They did not want their mother to be exposed to the virus. Cancer patients were especially vulnerable to it, and Kunal and Nandni were taking all precautions to keep Usha and her husband safe.

"I have informed uncle about her health. He wanted to come and meet, but I asked him not to because of the pandemic. He did seem to be bothered, but what else could I have done."

The siblings were close-knit, but the pandemic had blurred distances. Even the closest relative wasn't being able to come and meet their loved ones. The pain and consternation that accompanied such a circumstance bordered on inhumanity. The heart longed, and yet the fear of the infection was palpable. Usha has always been a social animal, and joy for her meant hours of conversation. Kunal and Nandni sometimes wondered about the source of her energy and excitement. Usha was also a pillar of strength and support for Nandni, who had her bouts of sadness. Usha would run her hand through Nandni's hair and give her a quick head massage. Her hands felt like Nandni's mother, and she would instantly rejuvenate. Daughters are always a soul closer to their mothers. The umbilical cord stays intact in the most symbolic manner. Nandni's connected with Usha's like a knot that can never melt even in the blazing fire that liquefies gold.

Nandni's day was scheduled to have a seamless routine of planned foods and medicines and exercise for Usha etc..; Nandni always had her legs fixed with ignited rockets that were always available for the needs of her husband, Usha, and the kids. Nandni was brimming with extraordinary talent, for she managed happenings perfectly. Kunal always took the time to appreciate Nandni for her patience and sincerity. She managed to send kids to school and their tuition classes without fail. But, amidst all, her primary attention remained on Usha... Where Usha used to give her support at times in making kids eat food and sleep... The bond between them was beyond what she could have felt for her mother. Nandni's love for Usha was like the gush of river water mixing with the vast and deep ocean, for it can never ever be disconnected.

The pandemic and the isolation thereafter had taken a heavy toll on everyone. While businesses floundered, lives too were getting grated through the sharp edges of fate. Kunal was still adamant that Usha would not be allowed to leave the premises for the check-up. Kiran and Kanchan were upset with their younger sibling but also understood the perils. The dichotomy of fate illustrated a classic conundrum that many countries worldwide failed to deny but desperately wanted to. There were sick and infirm who required medical help, yet the rapid spread of the disease and the ensuing lockdown proved to be debilitating challenges.

The months rolled by fast. Usha celebrated the birthdays of her daughters in November and December. It was quite a commemoration. Usha was, as usual, at the top of her game.

The festivities that follow such occasions are filled with fun and frolic.

She hugged her children and prayed to the Almighty for their long lives. This time appeared extraordinary since her children had quietly prayed for her well-being and long life. This exchange of wishes and prayers did certainly cause some uproar in the celestial kingdoms because Usha seemed to be doing better than when she was admitted to the hospital. However, the Ayurvedic treatment was holding on, and even though there were a lot of limitations, primarily regarding dietary habits, the fight was worth it.

The year ended, and Usha was excited about Christmas and the New Year. Most households in the country look forward to Christmas and the New Year. It is a time for celebrations, hope, and happiness, and Usha spreads loads of it.

"Best wishes for the new year," a radiantly smiling Usha would retort on the phone. Her warmth and enthusiasm reached far and wide. The telephonic conversations would turn into marathon gossip-mongering and a roll of laughter at the end.

Winters are chilly in Delhi. The weather reports mostly talk about cold waves, but Bhatia's residence was perennially on fire. The fire of wish and contentment.

"The new year will bring greater joy for my son, my lovely daughter-in-law, and my two gems."

Usha wasn't too expressive when it came to Ramesh. But when the souls are intertwined, one doesn't need words. The silence between the two smelled of love. They would look at each other and smile, and the two would hug. Partners of long do not require commonly endorsed actions to display affection. It flows naturally, and those oblivious to its existence would wonder how such relationships survive.

It did and how.

The whole family prayed hard for each other's well-being, focusing more on Usha and Ramesh. There was hope that the new year would bring in a better consideration, fastening their eyes tightly closed, wanting not to know the crash the following year might offer them.

I hope they say it is perfunctory. It depends on many factors, and the variables keep shifting objectives. There is no perfect definition of what hope surmises. The outer boundary of hope, too, is blurred, and there is little or no knowledge of how much ground it covers. Hope makes people cling to the last straw, even though the next big wave will likely be the last. No matter how marauding fate has been, hope lives on. The magic it creates within our hearts of us is exemplary and cannot be described by science or logic.

Hope has no logic.

But neither does time.

The new year bought in worst.

Nishok informed Kunal that Meena, their younger sister, was keeping unwell and had lost her appetite. This was going on for a considerable amount of time. Her kids finally got her tested and were shattered by what they received in the form of the result. Like her elder sibling, Meena had gall bladder cancer, and the prognosis was not positive. It was stage IV, and no one had any clue where it originated from and when it metastasized. Usha wasn't informed about it though Kunal rushed to Meena, whom he adored as much as his mother, and stood beside her like the eldest son and an elder brother to her children.

Nitin, Meena's son, has been running from pillar to post to get his mother treated at the best hospitals in the city. He was also open to options outside the capital city. But in vain. The doctors have been quite vocal and adamant in their brainwashing. Meena had no chance of survival, and they wanted her to be with her family in her final days. The family's desperation knew no bounds. As the news spread like wildfire on a windy day, relatives, friends, and well-wishers started thronging her house. Meena loved visitors, but this was overwhelming. Moreover, those who came to meet her got to know about Usha, too, and the recovery she had made.

This amplified hope.

Meena's house was close to Usha's, and the crowd would invariably start visiting the Bhatia residence now that they had come to know that the elder sibling was also suffering for a long time and was now battering. Kunal and Nandni had a tough fight at hand. While they loved the visits, this was awkward on two counts. First, the pandemic was raging, and they had to protect their parents from the ensuing contagion. While Usha, with her cancer, was susceptible to number One, Ramesh, too, hadn't been keeping well for years, and getting infected with Corona was the last thing their son wanted for them. Also, the siblings did not want their mother to know anything about her sister and her condition.

"Meena, too, has liver issues? Insane is the times. Pass on the telephone number of the doctor who was treating me for Nitin. He will cure Meena, I am sure." Said Usha to Kunal with a concern for her sister.

Kunal had created a wall of lies to veil Usha off any bad news. This carefully crafted subterfuge was meant to put up a show to the elderly lady, convincing her everything was fine even though the ship was sinking despite every measure undertaken to salvage it.

Meena was close to Usha and the two bonded over samosas, gossip, and their childhood. Fond memories were revived and exchanged. They would sit together for hours and reminisce about the days of yore. The infectious giggle of the oldies lightened Bhatia's residence. The current predicament of Meena was sudden, and her family wasn't ready for it. In hindsight, none will be. No matter how prepared we are for life, out of air comes something and our entire plan collapses, like a pack of cards, sabotaging our dreams one by one.

Kunal and Nandni played a significant role in keeping up the appearance. While they merrily engaged with their guests, Usha was kept out of every prying eye. The son knew that the visitors meant well but letting them near his mother would spell disaster. He, at every cost, wanted the Ayurveda treatment to work, and it was, he thought. His sisters were as worried about the current situation as their little brother. Meena was also close to Usha's children; they adored her as much as they did their mother. Masi was their favorite person, and she was unwell, sick with the same demon that slowly devoured their mother. The two sisters knew it was a simple liver disease that would require time but time! Are we blessed with it? Time is a limited asset, and there is never enough of it. The more we latch on to it, the faster it seems to flow.

Kiran strolled down her memory lane to the good old days, only to be left with tears. "You have thinned. You don't eat on time. Got checked by a doctor? How is your health?" were Usha's usual retorts whenever she met Kiran. The eldest daughter knew that her mother meant well, but the corporate world's stresses had rendered her less emotive.

Both the sisters visited their aunt the next weekend. She was lying on her bed in the second room on the ground floor of their house. The room had no windows and was choc a bloc with people. Seeing her nieces, the frail lady spread her arms out and radiated a great smile.

"My beloveds. How are you both?"

They hugged their aunt though they initially wanted to keep a safe space lest there spread infection. Then, holding their hand, Meena pulled herself up and sat, the pillows supporting her back.

"How's my sister?" was her immediate question.

"She is not well. Mom misses you a lot." Kanchan choked, not being able to hold back her tears.

"She will recover soon. Just don't tell her about cancer. She will start worrying needlessly."

They nodded.

"You, too, need to get well soon. How can this continue any longer?" Kiran, too, had tears in her eyes. It was beautiful to know that years of professional strife had not killed her soul.

Those tears mattered.

"Why are you crying? I am doing good barring the medications and the weakness."

They smiled faintly, and a momentary peace stayed amid them for a while.

The sisters stayed with their aunt for almost two hours.

"When would we meet again?" quizzed Meena.

"Only when you recover fully. With the pandemic looming large, meeting often is not good."

Little did the sister know that this was the last time they met her.

Kanchan called Usha the next day to tell her about their meeting with Meena. The mother felt relieved that Meena was able to talk to her children. She also felt nice that her younger sister remembered her fondly and missed her greatly.

"My best friend from childhood, she is." Usha recollected it with immense joy while talking about Meena.

Meena's health worsened, and the doctors announced no hope left... It was another round for the hordes of relatives to descend upon Meena's house to say their final goodbyes, but Nitin politely requested them not to since he wanted to spend time with his mother alone.

Kiran along with her husband, Vineet was on her way to her aunt's place when she got the message from Nitin and then proceeded toward Bhatia's residence.

"Didi, where are you?" Kanchan enquired.

"On the way. I am coming home. Nitin said that his mother

is sleeping right now, so we might go later and meet."

"Ok. The rest is also headed here." Kanchan sounded cautious.

The relatives who denied meeting Meena had begun pouring at the Bhatia residence since the houses were nearby. Kunal did not want Usha to get anxious and requested her to move up to the third floor while he and his wife gracefully attended to all the guests. Kanchan gave her mother company. Lunch was served, and pleasantries were exchanged. The wishes for their mother were accepted with open hearts. The siblings were in a dichotomy. On the one hand, their masi(aunt) was gradually slipping into the land of darkness, on the other hand, so many guests at the house meant there could be a potential spread of disease.

"Yes, Nitin, tell me." Nitin's phone call came as a blessed interlope, giving Kunal a break from the heedless crowd.

He listened to the caller with rapt attention, not uttering a single word. When asked about the call by Nandni, Kunal gave an empty glance and announced Meena's death with an emotionless face. They had loved Meena as much as they had their mother, and her loss was indefinable. Most tragedies are. They cannot be explained or described. It is just one gigantic void that starts swirling and expanding. . Deaths are always sudden and unacceptable.

"It's already so late. Where are you going?" Usha asked Kunal, who was getting ready to leave for his aunt's funeral.

"Masi's(aunt's)house. Nitin has asked for medicine. I will go it to him." Kunal answered in a somber voice.

The cremation ground was filled with their relatives. The siblings were present with their respective spouses. As the flame rose to the rising of the Sun and the stars above gradually waned against the burning pyre, it was already the beginning of a new day.

"How is your mother?" was the common ask.

Kunal began to feel uncomfortable, not just with the question but also with the realization that his mother, too, was fighting a difficult battle. He tore himself from the crowd as those questions did not express concern but instead instilled terror and fear.

Chapter

10

The Farewell

Chapter 10
The Farewell

Usha was gradually sinking. The visible signs were prominent. She had no clue about Meena's predicament and would keep asking Kunal about her. Kiran's heart sank when she saw her mother in such a state.

While she entered the second floor, Kiran found her mother standing in front of the mirror and touching her face.

She immediately hugged her and asked what she was doing.

"I look so old now. Can the doctor make me look young again?"

Both shared a quick look in silence before Usha started to puke. Kiran held her feeble hands and slowly took her towards the bedroom.

"You need to rest. Let's sit."

"I am tired of sitting. I sit and lie the whole day. I have little energy to stand too. I vomit often. These medicines have bad side effects."

"I will talk to the doctor. Meantime, have some coconut water." Kiran Responded to her mother

Kiran discussed their mother's failing health with Kunal and

Nandni. The couple was concerned about Usha's inability to digest food anymore.

Kunal consulted with the Ayurvedic doctor, who recommended cleaning the stent, placed in her liver. This had to be done through the hospital. The doctor also reduced the Ayurvedic dosage to facilitate better digestion of the medicines.

Kunal also discussed with Kanchan, and the sisters agreed in unison that their mother must be taken to the hospital immediately.

Kunal insisted that she be checked at home, after which he would take the reports to the hospital and show them to a specialist.

After going through the whole-body check-up that Usha had undergone at home, the doctor recommended that the stent inside the liver be replaced since there was a high probability it might have been blocked.

Though medical science does provide enough space for it, hoping against hope seemingly has a narrow window. It also closes extremely fast. A miracle, in any form, is a wish that mostly doesn't occur. Billions of ardent prayers swim around in the ocean of hope, a majority sinking without a trace.

Kunal was hesitant because of the rising cases of Covid and the rampage of the second wave.

With Holi around the corner, the locality and the city were gearing up to celebrate it with fervor and gaiety. However, the siblings lost all color within their hopes, seeing their mother deteriorate by the day.

On Holi morning, Kunal found the second-floor bedroom

empty. On further inquiry, the house help informed him that the elderly lady had slept on the 1st floor.

Kunal rushed down to find Usha, an early riser, lying unconscious and her mouth filled with vomit. He had no clue how long she was lying in such a state.

Shocked beyond comprehension and beginning to panic, Kunal called out for Nandni, who came rushing by. Kunal carried Usha to the second floor while Nandni cleaned her up and changed her clothes.

By that time, the nurse had come. She, without any further hesitation, had Usha put on inter-venal glucose. She gradually regained consciousness and found Ramesh, Kunal, Nandni, Kanchan, and Rahul staring at her with sullied and anxious eyes.

"What happened?" She was puzzled by the sudden change in circumstance.

"You fainted, mom. Do you remember anything?" Kunal quizzed.

"I only felt puckish and had called out to both of you, but I guess my voice did not reach you all."

The son couldn't hold back his tears, overcome by the guilt of not being able to respond to his mother's plea. The heartbreak was slow and stabbing.

Kiran and Vineet had rushed and were shattered to find Usha in such a state.

The second wave was tearing societies globally. Near and dear ones weren't allowed to say their final goodbyes to those who had lost their lives. The bed shortage was hitting countries hard, and Delhi was in no better position. Most of the hospitals had been converted into Covid Centers.

Kunal desperately looked for a medical contact, but none was forthcoming. Finally, the family doctor suggested that she be taken to the same emergency ward where she had earlier been operated on.

While a reference to the doctor was earned, taking Usha to the hospital would be more than an arduous task. The second wave was at its peak. Delhi was at the Centre of large-scale loss of human lives. The hospital had been turned into a Covid Centre with patients, anxious relatives, and harried medical professionals jostling space with occupied body bags. The sheer rush of people unnerved Kunal, who was initially hesitant to take Usha. However, the constant pestering of the sisters and the sudden loss of appetite of his mother broke his resolution.

The next night Kunal and Kanchan took Usha to the hospital. The latter repeatedly instructed Usha to keep her mask on to prevent any further affliction.

Kanchan held Usha's hand while Kunal completed the formalities. The hospital ward was divided into pandemic, and non-pandemic and specialized areas were demarcated as such. The spread of infection was said to be widespread; hence, the authorities were at their wit's end trying to figure out the best possible arrangements. The usual reception was shifted to a different place, and Kunal was now running corridors to get his mother registered for the check-up.

The emergency ward was packed with bedridden patients... lacked vitality.

After much effort and sweat, the registration was done, and the three sat at a corner of the second-floor corridor. The crowd was sizeable, and the siblings were anxious, watching it grow by the minute.

The on-call doctor ultimately assigned a bed to Usha... Kunal and Kanchan eventually permitted her to sit there.

Next to Usha's bed was a woman in her early 30s sleeping while her husband was howling and demanding doctors...

How come she died of Corona when she was brought in for a routine check-up?

Unable to bear the cacophony of tears and broken hearts, they decided to take Usha back to prevent her from getting overwhelmingly stressed.

They returned two days later after the doctor had provided Usha with a bed in the non-Covid VIP ward.

The fifth-floor non-covid ward was devoid of patients, and Usha was only one of the two.

Immediately upon admission, she was operated upon, and the stent in the liver was replaced. However, her condition did not change much, and the vomiting persisted.

Nandni was entrusted to look after her mother-in-law, while Kunal would look after Ramesh and his kids.

But the son wanted to be by his mother's side throughout the day.

To keep her engaged, Kunal began to play the games they used to play when he was a little kid of four.

With no signs of improvement, Usha was operated upon

once again, and a stent was inserted in both sides of her liver and as well as in a food pipe. This took a heavy toll on the frail body.

Usha, too, gradually began to give up. The 67 kgs.' of hale and heartiness had now reduced to 46 kgs.

The doctors finally announced to the youngest child of Usha that cancer had now significantly spread, and there was nothing more they could do. Kunal stared blankly, not ready to accept.

Kunal could hear the world shatter around him. The din of the chaotic ward had suddenly gone mute. He thought he could listen to his heartbeat too. The words of the doctor echoed through his mind repeatedly. The expected miracle was not to happen.

After an excruciating 25 days, Kunal brought Usha back home.

She could not carry her body weight, and Kunal immediately arranged for a caretaker, Preeti, who would look after their mother throughout the day.

Nandni got busy managing Usha's diet, and their sole aim was to get her back on her feet and restart the Ayurvedic medicines.

Kanchan was mainly at her mother's place, and they would chit chat for hours. She would also nicely comb Usha's hair and tell her stories about her beauty. Nothing interested her anymore.

On the morning of 27th May, a Thursday, Kunal called both the sisters. When asked why Kunal said he wasn't feeling right.

The fear of losing their mom hung heavy on his heart. It had now taken the shape of a monster.

Both the sisters, along with their spouses, arrived. The air seemed to be heavy, and there was a certain sadness that crawled through the walls. The house seemed to understand the circumstance that would gradually unfold in the immediate future. Walls are living organisms. They bear the sound of the memories that get created within its fold.

Usha was sleeping on the 1st floor. Vineet woke her up. Seeing her family around her, she quizzically asked when they had come. Then, slowly pulling herself out of the bet and slumber, she sat, even though words were barely coming out of her mouth. The daughters joined in the conversation. Vineet and Rahul sat in the drawing room, unable to bear the pain they saw their mother-in-law was suffering from.

Hunger was the last thing that was on the mind of anybody, though Nandni insisted they all eat something.

"Mom, come and sit with us. You will feel better." Kanchan softly requested the weak-bodied Usha.

She wasn't willing but did not want to miss out on the chance of being with her family.

However, it was short-lived. Soon after she sat, Usha wanted to return to bed.

"I am not feeling well today," Preeti was told.

"I am not being able to sit, nor sleep. The heart seems to be restless. I don't know what's happening."

Kiran, Vineet, Kanchan, and Rahul left in the evening.

"Just call whenever you need anything," they instructed Kunal.

The intense stomach pain started to stab Usha immediately after. The nurse gave her a shot of pain killer, which eased the agony. Preeti called Kunal.

"Beta, I am hungry." Usha Said as she saw Kunal...

Kunal was elated. In his broken world, this was the hope he was praying for. There was indeed some light, a flicker, maybe, at the end of the dreaded tunnel.

Usha has shown hunger after a considerable period.

He gave her lentils and coconut water, after which she wanted to go to the washroom.

While returning, she crashed. The body could no longer hold its weight.

Kunal laid her on the bed.

She stared at the ceiling and started to talk to herself. Kunal couldn't fathom what the conversation was. Scared at the end of his wits, he dialed a common video call to his sisters and begged them to come over immediately.

"Mom, who are you talking to?" Kunal wept inconsolably as he tried to reason.

Kanchan and Rahul reached and were aghast at seeing the helplessness in the room.

Understanding the trepidation of the situation, one of the neighbours joined as well.

Kanchan asked Kiran to come over as fast as possible.

The priest who was called had suggested that she be taken to the first-floor room.

Usha knew time wasn't on her side anymore. It is on no one's side. Time is a traveler, and we are its fellow passengers. The clock ticked as it always had. The children of Usha and her husband begged it to slow down. It was not to be bothered. Usha laid her head over Kunal's lap and waited for her daughter to arrive.

She kept murmuring and was almost out of breath when Kiran and Vineet arrived. Her eyes were flooded with tears, constantly flowing sideways, wetting her collided hair but avoiding her thin, wrinkled cheeks. Her painful murmurs echoed the room, uttering her silent words, "I don't want to go... I still want to live... I still have so much to do in this world...."

The grief-stricken entourage was asked to put basil water in her mouth. Kunal's tears won't stop. He had never seen his mother so helpless, and neither did he imagine he would see her like this.

The family finally, gathering all their strength, requested Usha to let go and leave to save herself from the pain. Ramesh's voice was the loudest.

"Go, my love. I will look after our children. And don't worry, I will join you soon."

The priest chanted while her breath eased out.

Kunal closed her eyes. Bhatia's residence had fallen silent. Usha left, taking her extraordinary experiences with her. Her wings were wide open, and the night sky looked brighter today.

Chapter

11

The Abiding Legacy

Chapter 11
The Abiding Legacy

The pink petal sky bridle with the softest accents of white was unusually delightful today, for the birds were waiting to open their wings and fly. Meanwhile, down in a narrow three-storied house, Kunal and Nandni were looking through Usha's 50-year-old Godrej almirah. Which could be best known as a preserved relic, painted for revival year after year since Usha's marriage, still stands tall and robust as if it came straight out of a TV commercial.

Nandni's trembling hands on the handle were revealing another tale. Even in her wildest dreams, she could not picture opening this almirah without the careful supervision of Usha, who is watching her movements like a hawk, but in a matter of months, the wheel of fate has spun, and now, she is the one who holds the keys. She has become the woman of the house. Yet, her heart still couldn't gauge this massive transition that had altered the dynamics of the household. While she stood there with her hands on the handle contemplating her actions, little Gauravi came peering through and shouted with all her being, "Don't touch my grandmother's almirah! She'll scold you when she comes back." Gauravi, for as long as Nandni could remember, would always be latched beside Usha, her little hands clinging onto her grandmother's wrinkly ones. Nandni felt bad for her; she couldn't even grasp that her grandmother was never coming back.

Nandni looked at Gauravi with bittersweet tears and said, "Grandma is watching over you even if she might not be able to come back." Then, another wobbly voice came through; this time, it was little Gatik who innocently exclaimed, "Mummy, *gandi baat hoti hai almirah touch karna, Dadi ne mujhe bola tha ki who meri shaadi mein aayengi.*"[82] She gazed at them both, biting back her tears as she smiled with affection at their innocence. It was strangely comforting to see that the harsh realities of the world haven't tainted their young minds yet, their innocent predispositions untouched by corruption.

Directing her focus back to the task at hand again, Nandni twisted the handle and found an organized bundle of sarees, intricately designed, a few pieces of jewelry and some other belongings stacked perfectly. Her mother's perfume suddenly reached her nostrils, and she could feel her all over again. The dewy floral aroma brought in waves of nostalgia. It felt like her mother lived in that almirah, which reflected her meticulous personality. Her aura was still fresh there, blessing their lives as she did when she was alive.

Suddenly, her eyes fell on the locker; after spending a few minutes in Usha's shoes, she still couldn't think of the perfect place for a pair of keys. Where could Usha have kept them? She started to look around, poking her palms in between the sarees and reaching all the far corners of the almirah. In doing so, she

---

82 Mom, it's wrong to touch someone else's almirah. Granny told me she would come to my wedding.

created a beautiful mess of the organized entity, but still, to no avail, the key stayed hidden from her desperate eyes. Finally, heartbroken, she called for Kunal, who tried to shift some sarees to look for the key. Still, Nandni told him anguishedly, "My dear, I've turned the whole almirah upside down, and I doubt the key is here."

Just at that moment, Kunal remembered his mother's words, "The key to the locker is only meant for you, Kunal." So, with a deep conviction, Kunal set out to look for the key again, that's when a turmoil of emotions hit him like an avalanche, and a solemn tear fell down his cheek... While shifting a few sarees and putting his hand through them to search for the key, he almost fell into his hands by some divine intervention. Everyone was shocked by how easily Kunal found the key to the locker.

"I searched for it everywhere," Nandni confessed.

"It was meant to be found by me," said Kunal, slightly dazed.

Unlocking the locker, Usha's belongings were distributed amongst her family members carefully so as not to disturb the divine entity that was going to live through her carefully carved sarees, her dainty jewelry, and a bundle of 50Rupees notes meant for her husband. With trembling hands, Kunal picked up an additional pile of notes, oddly 40 thousand rupees inscribed on them 'for anyone in need." He recalled how her mother was thoughtful and always willing to help others selflessly and wholeheartedly, a virtue seldom seen these days.

Kunal handed the bundle of 50 Rupees notes to Ramesh. He felt it, and as if instantly feeling a connection, as the Chinese myth goes, some people are connected through invisible red threads, and though they may be tangled but are never lost and the relationships always stay, to Usha he exclaimed. *"Usha main isse apne marte damm tak apne saath rakhunga[83]."* Kunal found a diary among these belongings which said *'Meri Kahaani[84].'* Not much of a keen reader, he thought about his sister, Kiran, who once gifted his mother 'The Power of the Subconscious Mind.' So, 'Meri Kahani' was handed to Kiran with a rustic black leather cover. A hastily scribbled 'Usha' inscribed on the first page made Kiran's lips instantly steal a smile of recognition, for she knew that her mother was as eager to tell her story as she was to say it to her's. But instinctively, her reflexes made her close the cover right away as she wanted to read her mother's diary in comfortable solitude and not in the hustle and bustle of an Indian household. Hence, she went and kept the diary safely in her black leather purse and made sure to close the zip.

In the evening, Kiran chose the perfect spot; after looking around and noticing that no child was in her vicinity, she tiptoed to the balcony. With mixed feelings, she decided to glance up at the sky, which was blanketed in an unusually itchy dark inky color and jeweled with stars that glowed like glass. Filled with grief and curiosity, she thought about how she'll watch Usha spread her wings and fly with her individuality now that she was the main character and Kiran had the first-class tickets for a movie she always watched from afar. She wanted to hand out those tickets to everyone else so they could witness Usha's life closely unfold through the years.

---

83 Usha, I'll keep this safe with me till my last breath.
84 My story

She took a deep breath and flipped the page, searching for her mother in between the commas and the full stops, her eyes scanning the words with hunger. Though she found herself, her mother's wounded wings needed revival. She knew from experience that opening your wings was not enough. Like tiny chicks, you must dive headfirst to have an endless flight. As she was flipping the pages, she could feel Usha's whole story taking life in front of her eyes, and at that moment, she knew her life's sole purpose was to help others find their wings.

Somewhere during the night, the whole day's weariness had caught up with her, and sweet sleep had fallen over her eyes. The night finally gave way to the first rays of sunlight that struck Kiran's heavy and teary eyes. With the book still in her hand, she managed to find a comfortable position to dream. Still, as the night gave way to the first rays of sunlight that struck Kiran's heavy and teary eyes, she stirred, waking up from her slumber. Rubbing her eyes while she roused herself awake, she managed to regain some consciousness of the surroundings in spite of being worn out by the activities of the previous day. Just then, the sun's rays guided her eyes to the last words that Usha had written, **'Usha ki Kiran.'**

Words From the Author

At this moment, I realized that I am just a messenger in the larger scheme of things. Whatever I am today is not because of me; it's just because I am Usha ki Kiran and that's the only name I want to be known by. She made me open my wings so that she could fly through me, and her ray of hope could fly through the people who needed someone to show them that no matter how dark their days turn, things will turn around for the better. Light will find them again... Usha, my beloved mother, lived a wholesome and happy life and made her children find their wings by lauding them with unconditional love because she knew how it felt for a child to be devoid of their parent's love and affection.

Still carrying her memory in my heart, I wrote her story. All along, it was her story, and I was the side character whom she made me into such a loving, courageous human being by giving pieces of herself to me in inheritance. Like an artisan, she shaped me to be capable of showing love to others and holding the capacity to understand the high and low tides of life.

Her life lessons and love keep me going. It's beautiful how human beings love making hearts, even if it's at the margins of their books or through their hands. We're so fond of love that it oozes out of us through such physical manifestations, and this love never runs out. Even when humans fall short of words to explain the feelings in their hearts, love has a way of transcending all physical and material boundaries. It slips past the black ink on paper and lives through what you feel when you read what I have written.

All that I wanted to say is that your story neither begins from the first page nor will it end with the last page... It flows through every human it touches, like a tranquil stream of water, and gives them wings. We are like caterpillars, unaware of our tainted glass wings and the potential we hold. Like butterflies, we fly, underestimating our worth, believing ourselves to be ordinary, while the encapsulated truth is that we live extraordinary lives.